THE POWER OF TWO

You are so there.

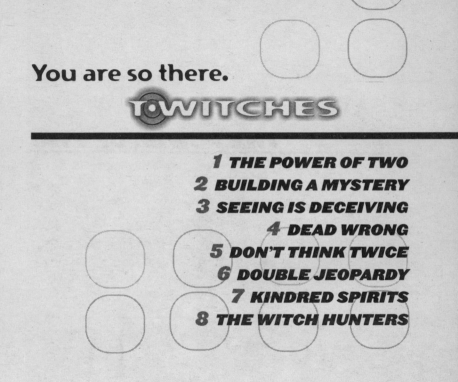

1 THE POWER OF TWO
2 BUILDING A MYSTERY
3 SEEING IS DECEIVING
4 DEAD WRONG
5 DON'T THINK TWICE
6 DOUBLE JEOPARDY
7 KINDRED SPIRITS
8 THE WITCH HUNTERS

T·WITCHES

**H.B. GILMOUR
& RANDI REISFELD**

SCHOLASTIC
NEW YORK   TORONTO   LONDON   AUCKLAND   SYDNEY
MEXICO CITY   NEW DELHI   HONG KONG   BUENOS AIRES

ISBN 0-439-54410-6

12 11 10 9 8 7 6 5 4 3 2 1   3 4 5 6/0

PRINTED IN THE U.S.A.

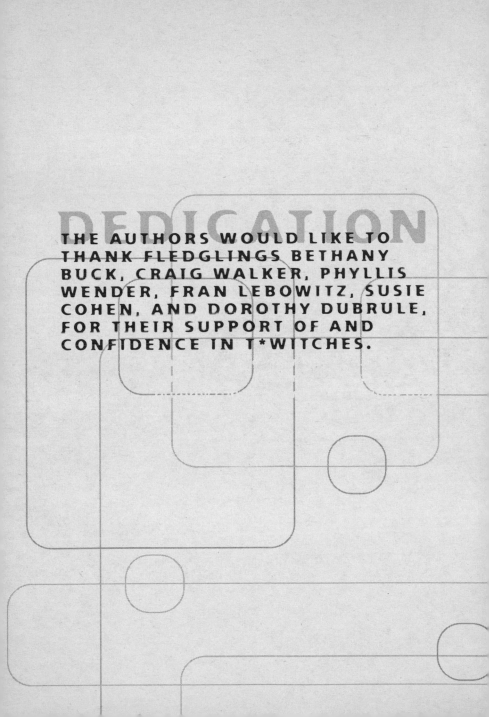

DEDICATION

THE AUTHORS WOULD LIKE TO
THANK FLEDGLINGS BETHANY
BUCK, CRAIG WALKER, PHYLLIS
WENDER, FRAN LEBOWITZ, SUSIE
COHEN, AND DOROTHY DUBRULE,
FOR THEIR SUPPORT OF AND
CONFIDENCE IN T*WITCHES.

CHAPTER ONE
FOURTEEN YEARS AGO

The midnight forest bristled with witches. A dozen or so ran through the moonlit grove, holding torches, searching, following their leader, the powerful warlock Thantos.

Another witch, young, vain, and beautiful, hid in the shadow of an ancient tree. Her name was Ileana. In her arms, two babies slept, pressed against her blue silk robe.

Her partner, the aged warlock Karsh, dressed all in black, from his velvet trousers and fitted waistcoat to his velvet slippers, seemed to have disappeared.

"Karsh," Ileana whispered, her breath visible in the icy night. "Coward. Why did you leave us?"

"Quiet," a voice commanded. It seemed to have come from the tree itself.

"I should have known," Ileana hissed, kicking the tree trunk. "Karsh, you old trickster, this is no time to show off."

"Shut up," the tree urged, adding politely, "oh, great witch."

Ileana was tempted to kick the trunk again, to whisper something rude at its scaly bark. But one of the babies began to wriggle in her arms.

The infant girl was very alert. Clearly, she sensed what Karsh had heard. Now Ileana could hear it, too. The heavy, hobnailed boots of the warlock Thantos crunching through the snow. The mighty tracker was leading his searchers toward them.

Quickly, Ileana dipped a finger into the herb pouch she wore around her waist, then brushed the honey-and-thyme potion across the stirring child's lips.

Which baby was it, Apolla or Artemis? They looked so alike, it was impossible to tell. Already their nearly colorless birth eyes were turning gray, the same startling gray as her own, Ileana noted.

As Thantos's footsteps drew nearer, Ileana saw the glint of one of the gold charms that helped tell the infants apart. It was the delicate half-moon necklace that belonged to Artemis.

Ileana should have known. Artemis was always alert, aware, attentive. Her twin sister, Apolla, whose necklace carried a different but matching charm, was the calmer of the two.

Of course, Thantos wanted these babies. Already their sensitivity was obvious. Their hearing was becoming honed. Their recognition of danger sharp.

But the mighty tracker and his torch-bearing mob ran right past them. Their footsteps grew fainter as they moved out of the woods.

Thantos had not found them. Still, Ileana pressed the infants to her, willing them not to cry out, not to make a sound.

Time passed — minutes, hours. Ileana waited, listened to the whirling wind, the hooting of a lone owl. Finally, she stepped out of the shadows.

"Karsh," she grumbled. "You can materialize now. We're all very impressed with your cleverness."

"Yes, great witch," he said.

Great witch? She is a child herself, Karsh thought, picking splinters of ice from his nappy white hair. Ah, well. The young deserve respect, need it to grow strong. Brushing snow from his velvet coat, which only a moment ago had been twisted tree bark, Karsh smiled.

Karsh was very old, an aged warlock, so practiced at his craft that he — like the forceful Thantos — had attained the rank of tracker.

He'd had decades to perfect his skills and senses.

While Ileana, for all her pouting vanity and temper, was but a guardian. She wasn't a bad witch, just young, willful, and terribly impatient.

Like all trackers, Karsh was a talented shape-shifter. It was not bragging to say he could turn himself into just about anything: a tree, a rock, flowing water, leaping fire, spiraling smoke, and animals and humans of every age and appearance.

Whereas Ileana had only been appointed the infants' guardian to humble her, to teach her to be reliable, responsible, trustworthy. To think of something besides her own youth and beauty.

"Take the babies, Karsh. Run fast and far. Find them protectors. Hide them," she commanded, throwing back the hood of her silk robe. "And don't call me witch." Ileana's gray eyes narrowed menacingly. "It sounds so common. I prefer goddess, or lady."

Now fully himself again, with only stray scraps of bark freckling his velvet waistcoat, Karsh stood before Ileana, as tall, thin, and agile as a willow branch. His wild white hair silver in the moonlight, he bowed slightly. "A thousand pardons, Lady Ileana."

"Make it goddess," Ileana decided, staring brazenly at his pale, bony face, which children often found frightening. "These babies must never know the truth of their power. Separate them, Karsh. Fling them far apart so that Thantos may never find them."

"Goddess, Lord Thantos —" Karsh spoke of the one who'd come closest to finding them.

"Lord of worms and beetles —" Ileana hissed.

"And wild ambition."

"That miserable tracker —"

"Excuse me?" Karsh straightened abruptly. "You're forgetting that I'm a tracker."

Ileana sighed impatiently. "How could I forget that? You don't stand still for a second. You're always showing off, shape-shifting and playing the brilliant trickster. But Thantos is a rebel, a renegade who calls up his magick for harm. I won't let him use these precious babies to feed his own ambition."

"He *is* their uncle," Karsh pointed out.

"He *killed* their father!" Ileana shot back. "Here, help me remove their amulets." She gave Karsh the serene infant Apolla, who was wearing the golden half-sun charm.

"Think, great witch —"

"Goddess, Karsh." Unlatching the half-moon necklace from Artemis's tender throat, Ileana sighed.

"But the babies . . . without their amulets, how will they know that each is one-half of the other?"

"They must not know." Ileana handed Karsh the half-moon necklace. The pale tracker accepted it, slipping the delicate charm into his vest pocket. When the time came, restless, young Artemis would wear it again.

But when Ileana wasn't looking he only pretended to remove her peaceful twin Apolla's half-sun charm. Ileana was trying to calm Artemis. "They must never know," she declared, rocking the wriggling child.

"Think . . . goddess," Karsh tried again. "Separately, they may one day be talented, accomplished, even remarkable practitioners of the craft, but only together can they attain their full powers."

"Exactly," Ileana said. "So long as they appear merely gifted, they'll be safe. But if they display their true wisdom and strength, Thantos will track them down and try to use their power for evil."

"They'd never allow it," Karsh reasoned.

Ileana whirled suddenly, her midnight blue cape flaring. "Then he'd kill them," she said.

CHAPTER TWO
CAMRYN

"Kill them!"

On the soccer field, Camryn Barnes, ace offensive player of the Marble Bay High School Meteors, heard the bloodcurdling cry from the stands.

Don't look, she told herself.

A shock of auburn hair had escaped Cam's ponytail and was sticking to her flushed cheek. Brushing it back fiercely, she forced herself to stay focused on the game.

It was too big to blow — the final match of the year, her freshman year of high school. And her crew, the Meteors, were so going to take the championship. Even if the Salem Wildcats, the toughest team in the league, were now leading by one point.

No way was some shrieking nutcase in the stands going to throw off Cam's game.

"Over here!" Dancing impatiently, she shouted to her best friend-slash-total confidante, Beth Fish. "I'm open."

"You've got it!" Beth hollered, her lanky legs shooting the ball sideways to her petite pal. At five feet four, Cam was three inches shorter than the rangy Beth.

"Do it, Cam. Kick it!" Kristen Hsu, one of the Meteors' guards, begged. "Now!"

Cam lunged for the ball, caught it on the run, spun, and sent it rocketing into the net. Scoring. Tying the game a second before the halftime whistle blew!

Then the whole team was racing toward her.

"You did it!" Beth, the first to reach her, threw her arms around Cam and started jumping up and down.

"We're just tied," Cam reminded her jubilant best bud, though she felt pumped and confident. "We've got another half to go."

"And then we are so out of here!" Beth squealed as they headed for the bench. "Vacations R Us. We're on for a monster week two thousand miles from Marble Bay!"

Don't go, Cam heard.

The voice was a rasping whisper that raised goose bumps. Cam looked around, rubbing her arms. Only Beth was near enough to have spoken so softly and been heard.

"Don't go where?" she asked Beth.

"Excuse me?" Beth blinked cluelessly at her.

"Didn't you just say we shouldn't go?" Cam asked, chilled suddenly.

"Nuh-*uh*." Beth shook her head, sending a frenzy of dark frizz bouncing. Between the tang of Marble Bay's sea air and the salty heat of the game, her naturally curly hair was bushing out like a Chia Pet on Miracle Grow. "No way. I'm totally up for this trip, remember? You, me, an awesome ranch —"

Don't go.

Cam heard it again.

This time she recognized the voice.

An icy breeze swirled around her, sending a shiver down her sweat-drenched back. Oh, no, she thought. Not now. Not in the middle of the most important game of my life.

How old had she been the first time? Seven or eight, she guessed, the first time she'd heard that scratchy voice, the first time she'd seen the bony man with the scary white face. She'd been afraid of him at first. The minute he disappeared, she'd run into the living room, almost tripping over her too-long pajamas. Her parents had company. Her dad was pouring coffee. "Yes, dear?" her mom had asked, scooping her up, smoothing back her hair.

The man, she said.

What man?

The skinny man all dressed in black.

A dream, her mom assured her.

No, no. I saw him. I heard him. He said my real name is Apolla.

She remembered it clearly, as clearly as she'd just heard the same voice say, *"Don't go."*

Brianna Waxman, who played left wing — if she hadn't broken a nail, or wasn't having a bad hair day — jogged over, yelling, "Meteors rule!"

"Excellent play." Kristen was ecstatic as she high-fived Cam.

"What?" Cam said. The buzzing in her ears had started. The dizzying hum she recalled from childhood.

"It was a dream, that's all," her mom had insisted. "Dave?" her mother implored him.

Her dad had taken her then, his big hands still warm from the coffeepot. He'd whisked her out of the living room, where she'd just announced, in front of company, that the necklace, the gold sun charm she'd worn since she was a baby, belonged to Apolla.

"Apple who?" one of her parents' friends had asked.

"A wise and beautiful witch," Cam had answered, according to her mom.

10 ―――――――――――――――――――――――

"Cam. Hello. Where are you?" It was Beth.

"Nowhere. Right here," she said, snapping back to the soccer field. "How amazing was that move? You couldn't have set it up better."

"Pure magic," Brianna cheered. "Cam's mojo is working overtime again."

Cam tried to laugh but only managed a weak smile. Ever since her fourteenth birthday, she'd been getting teased about her "mojo" — her sixth sense, the intuitions she had, the weird things she seemed to know before anyone else did.

She'd never told anyone about the pale old man, though. Except for Beth. Cam had told her when they were in fourth grade — even though her dad had said not to.

When he'd carried her back into her room that long ago night, he'd promised Cam that he believed her. Others might not, he cautioned.

He was right. Beth, her best friend even back then, hadn't bought it. "Yeeew, stop, Camryn," she'd demanded, covering her ears. "You're making it up. You're just trying to freak me out."

"Are you okay?" Beth asked now.

"Just got a little dizzy," Cam assured her. "Adrenaline rush." Her hand hurt. She was toying with her necklace, she realized, gripping the sun charm too tightly.

*   *   *

"Did you hear psycho Gladstone screaming in the stands?" Pulling off her red scrunchie, Kristen unfurled her gleaming black mane.

"Gladstone, as in Tonya?" Brianna — Bree — asked as they made their way to the team bench. "How could I not?"

"Was she the one who screamed, 'Kill them'?!" Beth asked.

"Who else?" Bree responded, rolling her eyes.

Tonya Gladstone, the girl they were talking about, was a misfit and a mystery. Two years ahead of them, she'd come into their school midsemester. It was now the end of June and although she *was* on their soccer team, she had remained a loner. The only thing anyone really knew about her was that her parents were mega-rich and always traveling.

Yet today, she was all spotlight-girl.

But then again, who wouldn't be, sitting right next to Marleigh Cooper, teen celebrity flavor-of-the-year? Bringing America's pop princess to the Marble Bay soccer finals, Tonya had just about managed to upstage the game.

How Tonya had ever gotten a singing superstar like Marleigh to come to their high school championship game was a total brain-boggler. The teen diva had the number-one song in the country right now. Her stream-ing blond hair and perfect white-toothed smile beamed from the covers of a dozen teen 'zines. Yet there she was, trendy wraparound shades protecting her baby blues, perched in the stands next to Tonya Gladstone.

"What happened to Tonya's leg?" Beth asked, mo-tioning to the bleachers, where a crutch stood propped against the bench next to her. "I didn't know she got hurt."

"No clue." Cam shrugged. "Until she showed up with Marleigh, I just assumed her sprained ankle kept her out of the championship game." Cam lowered her voice to a whisper. "You sure you didn't hear anyone say, 'Don't go'?"

"Say you're kidding," Beth begged. "Don't do this to me, Camryn. I hate when you get weird on me."

"Psych!" Cam said, as if she were joking and had just asked the question to fake Beth out. Then she quickly hid her face in the towel, mopped her clammy cheeks and forehead.

Inside, she fought a familiar stab of dread. Was she crazy, losing it, imagining things? She wished the answer was yes. It would be easier than being a freak, easier than knowing she was the only one who went through this stuff.

"And we've got to get a picture with our team's star and my *very* close friend, Camryn Barnes."

Cam spun around. Limping toward them, a crutch under one arm and the other wrapped around Marleigh Cooper's cashmere-clad shoulder, was Tonya and a photographer.

"Cami, hey, girl!" Tonya was glowing. "Meet Marleigh. I told her all about you."

Flustered, Cam said, "You did? I mean, hi. It's great you could make it to the game."

"I wouldn't have missed it." The celebrated teen, whose sizzling new video owned the airwaves, reached out to shake Cam's hand.

"Camryn and I are like this," Tonya gushed, crossing her fingers. "We're really tight, so we're definitely taking a picture with her. She's the most popular girl in the school."

Close friend? Really tight? What was she talking about? Cam blushed suddenly, embarrassed for Tonya.

Reality check: Tonya had no close friends. Maybe she should have been friendlier, Cam mused, but Tonya just sent out this weird vibe. Which was especially strong right now.

"Hi, Marleigh," Beth said, shyly stepping forward as Tonya hobbled over to the photographer to set up the shot. "I'm one of your biggest fans." Then she smacked herself on the forehead and went, "Yuck, how lame. I can't believe I just said that."

"This is Beth Fish," Cam did the awkward intro, "my . . . other best friend." She shot Beth a pleading look. "Beth should totally be in the picture, too."

"That last goal was awesome." Marleigh whipped off her wraparound shades and beamed at them. "I've never played soccer, but you guys make it look so fun."

"Really, you've never played?" Cam said.

"That, and a zillion other things I haven't done."

"I guess you've always been too busy — with your career, and, uh, doing this kind of stuff." Cam motioned toward where Tonya was giving detailed instructions to the photographer. "You must get invited to lots of things like this. It's really nice of you to come."

Marleigh frowned. "It's actually unusual for me to do this . . ." She lowered her voice. "I mean, the circumstances have to be pretty intense."

Pretty intense? What was she talking about?

"Okay," Tonya shouted as members of both teams gathered to watch. "Cam, stand on Marleigh's left, Beth, hold my place between them — I want to be sure there are no shadows." Tonya nudged the photographer aside so she could look through the lens herself.

Marleigh smiled at Tonya, then turned back to Cam. "Anyway, even though it's really tragic about Tonya . . ." She glanced up, searched Cam's eyes apologetically, as if she'd said too much, and continued, "These are really the best moments for me, when I can truly give something back. Because after all, these are the people who put me where I am."

Tonya? Tragic? Cam tried to figure that one out, but came up blank.

"Your fans, you mean?" Beth ventured. "It must be amazing to know so many people are into you and look up to you as a role model."

Marleigh grimaced. "Yeah, it's really great. Most of the time, anyway. Some of my fans are kind of, well, over the top. You wouldn't believe some of the weird fan mail."

"People asking you to come to their birthday parties and stuff?" Cam laughed.

"That doesn't bother me, that's kind of sweet, actually." Marleigh shook her head, as if trying to shake off a vibe. "Lately, there's this one shady creep who calls himself 'Devoted.' Demented is really more like it. . . ."

"More like what?" Tonya handed Beth her crutches to hold, then wedged herself between Cam and Marleigh and threw her arms around them.

"Nothing really. Marleigh was just saying how, uh, *intense* some of her fans are," Cam said.

"You mean like me?" A dark cloud scudded across Tonya's face. She glared at them, her eyes overcast with anger.

"Of course not," Marleigh assured her.

"Some guy," Cam quickly added. "Just some weirdo."

Tonya turned to the photographer. "Okay, we're ready now. Everything's perfect."

Later, when the picture was printed in newspapers across the country, Cam would notice that Tonya was the only one smiling.

CHAPTER THREE
A FACE IN THE CROWD

"The game's gonna get started in a second, Marleigh, we better go back to our seats," Tonya announced minutes later, when she was satisfied that the photographer had taken enough shots.

Beth extended her hand. "It was really cool meeting you. Maybe later, we can —"

"Yeah, right. Later," Tonya interrupted. Throwing her arm around Marleigh's shoulder, she started toward the bleachers. Not before the superstar glanced back at Cam and waved.

"What'd diva divine say?" Kristen strolled over with Brianna.

"Yes, what was your audience with Chica Plastica

like? Did she at least say something important — like where she got the cashmere wrap?" Bree faux-gushed. "As if I didn't know. I'm so all over that catalog."

Before Cam could answer, the whistle sounded for the second half. The Meteors took the field again.

"How cool is she?" Beth caught up to them. "I mean, wasn't she, like, so . . . I don't know . . . real?"

"Which part?" Brianna asked, all sugary innocence. "Her nose? It's definitely been done. Eyes? Custom contacts. And that blond-on-blond hair? Weave job."

"No way!" Beth protested.

"The ultimate brain-boggler is how Tonya got Marleigh Cooper here in the first place. It's not like *she* has any showbiz connections," Bree, whose dad was a Hollywood producer, asserted.

Beth shrugged. "I've heard that she hangs out with this kid who works at the Music & More store — maybe that had something to do with it."

Bree scoffed, "You mean the slacker who always wears that skull earring? As if he has any pull. He's a lackey."

"Anyone about soccer?" It was Kristen. "Eyes on the prize, girlfriends. It's gonna take some serious hustle to win this game."

"Which we are *so* gonna do," Cam promised.

The Salem Wildcats had other ideas. Thanks to

Lindsay Luckinbill, their top scorer, they managed to block every move the Meteors made.

Finally, near the end of the second half, Lindsay got between a pass from Kristen to Beth. Snagging the ball, the Wildcat star headed downfield with it. If she scored, Salem would break the tie — and take the game.

Cam was already on the case, racing after Lindsay, when Bree squealed, "Mojo girl, put the hex on her!"

Yeah, right, Cam thought, pounding behind the speeding 'Cat. *Slow down, Lindsay, so we can win. Blunder and stumble. Let the fun begin.*

Excuse me? Where had that come from, Cam asked herself, as Lindsay drew within kicking distance of the goal. When had she started thinking in rhyme?

Unexpectedly, Lindsay glanced over her shoulder, as if trying to see how far behind her Camryn was. It was a fatal mistake.

Cam was very close, near enough for her startling gray eyes to lock on to the Wildcat's green glare.

Lindsay skidded abruptly. Squinting, blinking, she twisted her head away from Cam's stare, her concentration broken. And, instead of kicking the ball, she tripped over it!

The girl did a total face-plant into the field.

And came up, with a blade of grass stuck to her cheek, completely ballistic.

"Foul! She blinded me!" Lindsay bellowed. "I mean . . . she tripped me! Barnes pushed me!"

I did? Cam zoned into total confusion as a time-out was called. Why else would Lindsay stumble and fall? No way could it have happened just 'cause Cam had *thought* about it — or *wished* she would.

Cam didn't protest. She couldn't. She had no clue what had just taken place. Except that the 'Cats were awarded an indirect free kick.

As Lindsay set up for her freebie, Beth trotted up to Cam, looking grim. "You didn't really push her, did you?"

Cam grimaced. "I don't . . . I mean, no. I would never do that. Right?"

Worried, wary, Beth studied her best friend as Lindsay's kick did its job: whacking the ball in the bucket, putting the Wildcats in the lead by one point.

The one point, as it turned out, they needed for the win.

Because, a few minutes later, with the ball back in play, rocketing toward Cam, and the field wide open for the cleanest, easiest goal anyone could have made, it happened again.

She heard the voice. His voice.

Don't go. It's too dangerous. She needs you now.

She? Stunned, Cam closed her eyes. Who needs her? Beth? Tonya? Marleigh?

Marleigh, she thought.

She's going to be snashed.

Snashed? What did that mean? Had she heard it right? Her eyes flew open. She turned toward the stands. A redheaded blur caught her eye. She honed in on the movement and saw a little girl, a carrot-topped kid no more than six or seven, rushing along the bleachers.

By the time Cam's gaze returned to the spot where the pop star and her fan club president had been cheering, Marleigh Cooper was gone.

But Tonya was still there, talking on her cell phone. Tonya and a lanky, bone-white man, dressed all in black.

Cam recognized his face. For years, it had been haunting her dreams. Now here it was, in her waking world — paper-thin skin, pasty pale. Deep sunken eye sockets stared straight at her. What was he doing here? What did he want?

Somewhere, far away, she thought her teammates were shouting, "Kick it, Cam! Boot it! Don't just stand there! Tie it up! This is the GAME!!"

But it was as if someone had pressed the pause button.

Cam stared, mouth agape, cold sweat streaming from every pore. Soaked, her scarlet jersey stuck to her ribs, but her mouth was dry as dust. No words came when she tried to scream.

Hundreds of shrieking fans in the stands, dozens of players on the field. Didn't anyone else see him? How could the dream face be here? Was she dreaming now?

A sickening feeling of frigid dread flooded through her again. Please, she wished, let it be my wild mind, let it be, like Mom says, my overactive imagination.

"Snap out of it, Cam! Now!" Beth Fish was in her ear, leading a shrill chorus of their teammates. "What are you waiting for? Do it! Kick!"

Cam tried to focus. She forced her attention back to the field. The ball was in position. Summoning all her strength, she willed her foot to fly out and send the ball hurtling toward the goal.

It never happened.

Frozen in place, Camryn Barnes, the player formerly known as Marble Bay's ace forward, was wide awake — and caught in the icy grip of a very real nightmare.

CHAPTER FOUR
ALEXANDRA

Artemis, arise! She needs you. Go with her.

As if carved of bone, a chalk-white face, all glaring planes and shadowy sockets, grinned at her.

Alex's eyes popped open. Sunlight blasted through the rust-stained, broken blinds of her cramped room. It stung her pale gray eyes. Dazed, she squinted against the glare.

She was drenched in sweat. Her choppy, blue-streaked hair, dyed to startle and offend, was soaked. Her heart thudded, pumping fiercely against the torn, now-soggy T-shirt she'd worn to bed.

The sheet beneath her was tangled. It gripped her ankle.

Where was she? Who needed her? Who was she supposed to go with?

Then she heard the strangled gasps, the wheezing, and she realized who needed her. She smelled coffee brewing and the bitter fumes of her mother's first cigarette of the day. And she knew she was home.

Home for Alexandra Nicole Fielding was the rented trailer she shared with her mom twenty-five miles from what passed for civilization in Crow Creek, Montana — the nearest McDonald's.

Hardy Beeson, the Fieldings' rancid landlord, called the leaky rust bucket a "modular dwelling." But the kids at Alex's school knew it for what it was.

"Trailer trash," Ina Barrow had called Alex and her friends. But she'd only said it once — in the gym, about nine months ago, right after Alex had turned fourteen.

She never would say it again.

Not after the basketball Ina had been holding leaped suddenly, sprang up out of Ina's own two hands, bloodying her nose, knocking Ina Barrow out cold.

That was when they'd started whispering that there was something weird about Alex, something witchy.

"Mom! Are you smoking?" Alex called. Then, sitting up abruptly, she smashed her head against the shelf above her narrow, built-in bunk.

Alex threw her hands over her head and ducked.

Books and magazines rained down, along with a couple of CDs and a clatter of cassettes. Last month's issue of *Teen People* — the one with Marleigh Cooper on the cover — tumbled into her lap.

Marleigh Cooper. White-blond hair. Blue eyes rimmed with thick black lashes. Skin flawlessly white over gently jutting cheekbones.

There was something about the young singer . . . something about the whiteness of her face, her white teeth, pale skin . . . delicate bones.

Alex remembered the dream face, the one she'd dreamed before, the skinny old man's face. His lively eyes buried in deep dark sockets, his voice a whispery rasp.

No way, she thought. The dream face was frail, ancient, scary looking. How could anything about Marleigh Cooper, who was only a few years older than Alex and famously beautiful, who seemed so nice, such a genuinely good person, remind her of that haunted grin?

Then the last book fell.

Luckily, it was a paperback. It bounced off Alex's head, tumbled over her protectively raised arms, and landed in her lap, eclipsing Marleigh's photogenic grin.

"Oh, nuts," her mom called, a chuckle in her raspy voice. "Did you get beaned by the shelf again? Are you okay?"

In a heap of books and bedclothes, Alex laughed. "I

asked you first," she hollered, then frowned, as her mother's gut-wrenching cough started up again. "Mom, you said you were quitting!" she called, picking up the paperback in her lap.

Myths and Magic of the Ancient World was the book's title. She'd checked it out of the library and had started reading it for a five-page report. Which, of course, she'd blown off.

But the book . . .

The book had been due back weeks ago! Great. She'd probably owe her entire minimum-wage salary in fines by the time she got it back to the library.

What was up with her? She'd gotten seriously spacey lately. Even her friends, all two of them, had noticed.

Evan, who worked with her at Big Sky, the bogus frontier "theme park," had developed the annoying habit of rapping on Alex's skull, going, "Hello, anybody home?" And her best bud, Lucinda, opened practically every other sentence with, "Girlfriend, are you with me?" Which was so getting on Alex's one last nerve.

And now she was having these whack dreams again. *Artemis, arise.* She had heard that grating voice before.

As clearly as she had heard Andy Yatz a couple of weeks ago.

Alex had passed the studly senior in the school hall the day after she'd gotten her long hair chopped and colored. She could have sworn he'd called her a babe. She'd recognized his voice.

Only Andy hadn't actually said a word out loud.

Lucinda, who'd been standing right there, had assured Alex of that.

Alex flipped restlessly through the library book, searching its pages. But, cadet that she'd become, she didn't have a clue what she was looking for.

The wracking cough began again, muffled this time. Her mother was probably holding a dish towel or something over her mouth. Without glancing up from the paperback, Alex yelled, "Put it out, Mom!"

Then she saw it. There it was in the book. The name — Artemis!

Artemis, she now remembered reading, was the goddess of the hunt, a fierce and vengeful warrior princess of the ancient world. But also a protector. Lady of wild things, the ancient Greeks had called her. Protectress of dewy youth. Animals and children were sacred to her. According to legend, Artemis ruled the moon, while her dazzling twin brother, Apollo, was guardian of the sun.

That explained it. Alex closed the book and got out of bed. She wasn't going mental after all. The name, the voice, she'd just had her weird dream again — only this time, she'd read about Artemis and incorporated the legendary goddess into her dream.

But, Alex thought as she shuffled out of her closet-sized room and started down the narrow hall toward the kitchenette at the other end of the trailer, that didn't explain how she knew what Andy Yatz was thinking. Or why a basketball she'd merely looked at while thinking hateful thoughts had wound up braining bigmouthed Ina Barrow. Or any of the other strange stuff that had been going on lately.

She'd started Crow Creek Regional this year. Was it the school? Was there something whack in the walls, like asbestos, that could cause weird things to happen?

She'd tried to figure it out before and, any way she looked at it, the answer was always the same. There was nothing wrong with the school. There was nothing menacing lurking in the building or hidden inside the puke-green walls. It was her. There was something hazardous in her.

Her mom was standing at the two-burner stove, scrambling eggs. And smoking, of course. Alex stood behind her, frowning, wishing someone or something could get her to quit.

The cigarette suddenly fell out of her mother's mouth and landed in the frying pan, sizzling. "What in the world?" her mother gasped. Then, glancing suspiciously over her shoulder at Alex, trying to hide a smile, she said, "Very funny. Cut that out."

"Don't look at me, I didn't do it," Alex vowed. Although it was exactly what she'd been thinking of doing, yanking the butt out of her mom's mouth and trashing it. "What time's your appointment?"

"At the clinic? Around three, I think." Her mother grabbed the crumpled dish towel lying on the chipped Formica counter and used it as a pot holder. "And you're not taking off from work, okay? I can handle this just fine by myself."

"Mom, I want to go with you. I had another totally weird dream —"

Fishing the soggy cigarette from the frying pan, her mother pointedly cut her off. "So what was that crash?" she teased. "Girl meets shelf again?"

All Alex heard was the wheezing between her mom's words. "Naturally. What else would it be?" She forced herself to sound cheerful, too. "I thought you asked Beeson to take it down."

"Hardy Beeson? Only about ten times. I'd do it myself if the bolts weren't so rusted. Your daddy would've had it off and out of here in five minutes."

Yeah, and if he hadn't split on us, Alex thought but

didn't say, we wouldn't be stuck in one of Beeson's over-priced tin boxes.

"Mom, let me go with you today." She quickly changed the subject. It had been more than six years since her dad, Ike Fielding, had left. She'd been barely eight years old. But she still didn't like talking about it.

They'd never exactly been rich, but things had gone downhill fast since Ike disappeared. The bank had foreclosed on their runty little house and people had come out of the woodwork demanding money they claimed Ike Fielding owed them. Even working two jobs — daytime at the laundry in town and nights at a greasy diner — her mom could barely keep up.

"How'd you become such a worrywart?" her mom asked cheerfully, as if she'd read Alex's mind. "I didn't rear you that way. And didn't you say Evan's driving you to Big Sky this morning?"

"Yikes, I totally spaced. He'll be here in ten minutes," Alex said, grabbing a piece of white bread from the bag on the table. "I'll phone you later at the laundry. You can have the eggs. I'm not all that hungry."

"Since when?" Her mother laughed. "You were born hungry."

"Oh, yeah, right. Is there any peanut butter left?" Alex stared in at the half refrigerator that sat under the counter.

It was pitiful. A pint of milk, a jar of jelly, a ball of wilted lettuce, two puckered tomatoes, and a just about empty jar of store-brand peanut butter.

Something was up. Her mom, Ms.-together-we-can-do-anything, was not taking care of business. However little money they had, there'd always been food — delicious, nutritious, lick-your-plate-clean food, and lots of it. Sara was positively witchy in the kitchen. She could turn Cinderella's coach into a pumpkin pie.

Alex grabbed the peanut butter and a spoon. She was leaning back against the counter, scraping the last lumps of peanut butter, when they heard a truck pull up.

"Is that Evan?" her mother asked.

Alex's nostrils flared as a rank odor assailed them. "No," she said, before she even peeked out the window.

A skinny man with leathery skin and two wisps of greasy gray hair plastered over his bare, sunburned dome climbed out of a shiny red pickup. "I knew it," she muttered. "Ugh. It's Hardy Beeson."

"Oh, no. I told him we're not paying a penny more for this place. He hasn't fixed one thing he promised to." Alex's mother began to cough again, so violently that she was bent double over the stove. She pressed the crumpled towel to her lips, trying, uselessly, to stifle the noise.

"Sit down, Mom," Alex ordered. "I'll talk to him. You just sit and rest now."

The metal trailer door rumbled as Hardy Beeson pummeled it with his fist.

Involuntarily, Alex sniffed the air. The sour stench of the man grew stronger — a smell of burnt animal, basted with gasoline and sweat. She recognized Beeson by it, the way a wisp of baby powder told her Lucinda was near, or the rich sweet smell of dark chocolate was Evan.

"Just a second," Alex called. Pulling the stool out from under their two-seater table, she eased her mother onto it.

With a grating squeal, the trailer's door screeched open. And there was old Hardy, his hand already reaching for the money he believed due him. "Now, Sara —"

"Why didn't you wait?" Alex demanded, the smell of him making her want to gag, making her dizzy. "I said, 'Just a second.' I didn't invite you in."

She set the peanut-butter jar down on the yellow Formica. The spoon still sticking out of it rattled, sounding nearly as irritable as she felt. "And don't call her Sara," Alex warned, turning to face the leathery landlord again. "She's Mrs. Fielding to you!"

Beeson ignored her. "We ain't gonna argue about a couple of dollars, Sara —"

The peanut-butter spoon, trashy aluminum with a cheap, red plastic handle, was suddenly sailing past

Alex's ear. Whizzing like a whole hive of hornets. *Ping!* It bounced smack off the middle of Hardy Beeson's wide forehead, leaving a big welt.

Hardy reeled backward, hanging on to the narrow door frame with two hands. Stunned, he shook his head gingerly, trying to come back to his senses — or the pure meanness he mistook for reason. "I'm finished with you two," he hissed, backing down the single step. "I'm finished tryin' to be fair." The door slammed shut behind him.

"Mom!" Alex gasped, astonished, shocked, proud. "That was awesome!"

"What?" her mother said, her voice muffled by the towel.

"The spoon. The way you hurled that sucker!" The words were hardly out of Alex's mouth when a sudden chill raised goose bumps on her pale arms and an alarming certainty bristled the hair on the back of her neck.

Her mother hadn't tossed the spoon. Her mother hadn't touched it.

CHAPTER FIVE
THE GROVE

Karsh was too impatient to wait for the ferry. With an effort that made his bones ache, the old warlock transported himself across the great lake.

The moment his boots touched Coventry Island, he found himself wondering if he had done the right thing.

The best way to reach young witches, he'd found over the years, was to let them know that some good soul needed their help. Their natural desire to be useful would do the rest.

Karsh had used this method to test the skills of hundreds of fledglings. He'd point them toward trouble and see what they could do.

None had ever come close to Apolla's and Artemis's

abilities. He'd seen Artemis deftly deal with a rude class-mate, and even though she did it quite by accident, Apolla blinded her rival in a soccer game, causing the player to stumble and fall.

So Karsh had tried to convince Artemis to stay close to poor Sara, and he'd hinted to Apolla that the celebrity was in danger.

But had he truly done all he could to carry out Ileana's wishes? Or had his stubborn belief that the young ones should never have been separated in the first place wormed its way into his intentions? Karsh mas-saged his throbbing temples as he hurried through town, scarcely aware of the greetings called out to him.

As one willing to die to save Aron's daughters, he had done what he thought best. As one pledged to serve their headstrong guardian, he'd probably fallen short. In truth, Karsh had to admit, this attempt to keep the girls separate had been halfhearted at best.

Had he placed them in harm's way, then? In Thantos's way? Was Ileana right? Did their desperate un-cle want them both or not at all? Did he want to harness their power to increase his own?

Of what possible use could the youngsters be to such a powerful man — a man who'd achieved bound-less success in the world beyond Coventry Island? A cap-tain of industry, a millionaire several times over?

It was impossible to know. The foul tracker had left the island long ago. Fourteen years ago, Karsh marveled, mere days after Karsh had found protectors for the infants.

Bees drifted lazily among the wildflowers lining the path to Ileana's cottage. Her orange cat, Boris, napped on the slate doorstep. Karsh stepped over the indolent creature and rapped at the cottage door. "Ileana, where are you?" he called dutifully.

There was no answer. I'll just leave her a note, he thought, relieved.

"Oh, for pity's sake," came a drowsy voice, "I'm here, in the forest, Karsh."

He heard her hammock creak as she stirred.

Shading his eyes, the troubled trickster gazed into the shadowy woods. "Still sleeping?" he called, spotting her.

"Well, I was." Ileana stretched lazily.

Karsh made his way through the herb garden, absentmindedly taking stock. He saw tender violets, which sweetened all about them; basil, known for bringing wealth; burdock for cleansing negative feelings; roses for use in love magic; purifying lavender, courage-inspiring thyme, peace-giving chamomile, and victory-enhancing laurel. The fragrant plants looked pleasingly lush. Even in his nervousness, Karsh was impressed by the bounty of Ileana's garden.

He wondered if she used fertilizer or incantations. A bit of both, he guessed, feeling surprisingly proud of her.

He, alone, was responsible for Ileana's training — as he had been for dozens of young witches and warlocks before her. He interfered only when she, or the course of action she chose, was dangerously wrong.

She'd come a long way in every area of her training, except social, Karsh lamented. Bright and beautiful as she was, Ileana was still vain, self-centered, and, well, disrespectful.

"Oh, no, don't tell me you've been out scaring children again." Her silvery laugh sealed Karsh's chagrin. "You're too ancient to go about with an unadorned face, old trickster —"

Karsh sighed. "I would not have been heeded in disguise today. I needed to be myself. I made an appearance. Two, actually. One physical, the other in a dream. While you, your witchness —"

"Goddess." Ileana yawned.

Arguing with the hotheaded Ileana was too tiresome, however. So he gave in to her silliness.

"Goddess, lady, your magickship, obstinate elf! Get up and get over yourself, Ileana. The children are in danger —"

"My babies? Both of them?" She sat up abruptly, blinking her steel-gray eyes. Though fourteen years had passed, Karsh thought, she looked no older than her charges.

"In danger of *meeting*," Karsh finished his sentence. "That's all I meant." He was tempted to say more, but what was the use? They'd been all through this. She believed they were safer apart; he'd always thought they should be together. But up until now, no harm had come to them. "Apolla is going west," he announced.

"West is a big place, Karsh," Ileana responded, annoyed but fully alert now.

"West to Montana," the old tracker explained.

"Whose bright idea was that?" Ileana swung her slender feet to the forest floor, brushing leaves and twigs from her peacock silk robe.

"Whose idea, indeed," Karsh said meaningfully.

"If this is Thantos's doing," she raged. "If he brings them to harm —"

"I tried to talk Apolla out of it," Karsh reported. "I warned her that her new friend would be snashed —"

"Snashed?" Ileana was waiting for an explanation.

Karsh grinned proudly. "It means taken, stolen. It's what they say these days."

"*Snatched!*" she corrected him. "Why don't you speak plainly?"

"I like to keep up-to-date on language," Karsh asserted. "I also alerted Artemis. Of course, it's possible that Lord Thantos is behind this. But it's also possible, oh, grumpy goddess, that the time simply has come. They have the power. They're already using it. Ah, but together, they'd be capable of so much more."

"Which is exactly why Thantos must not find them together," Ileana insisted.

"But if he did — and I'm just saying if — wouldn't their combined strengths serve them better than if each encountered him alone?"

"Thantos, that black-bearded, murdering hulk of a warlock, is a tracker, Karsh. A monstrously accomplished, shape-shifting tracker. The joined magick of two little girls, no matter how talented they are, could never defeat him."

"I've seen them." Karsh couldn't help smiling. "They're awkward and untrained, it's true, but also remarkably gifted. And, Ileana, they're not babies anymore."

CHAPTER SIX
A RANDOM DECISION

MARLEIGH STILL MISSING!

The headline of the *Montana Mountaineer* blared the shocking news.

From the front seat of their rented minivan, Cam's mother, Emily, read the story aloud. "It's been four days and still no sign of the young recording star who disappeared Friday from a high school soccer match in suburban Massachusetts."

"Unbelievable." At the wheel of the van, Cam's dad, Dave, shook his head. "A famous kid, a teenage celebrity, just vanishes in broad daylight. No one saw anything, no one heard anything — and still there's no sign? I'm not buying it."

But there had been a sign, Cam thought, leaning forward from the backseat to read over her mother's shoulder. The old skinny guy she'd seen in the stands, he'd tried to tell her someone was in trouble.

She needs your help, he had warned.

Or had Cam imagined it? Had she just flaked at the championship game, been flattened by stress, crumpled in the crunch? And what? Conjured up a scary old guy from her dreams who no one else seemed to have seen or heard?

"It's so surreal," Beth said, startling Cam. Chin propped on the backrest of the front seat, Beth absently twirled a strand of thick, curly hair. "I mean, we were there."

Emily Barnes turned to smile at them. "And now we're here. On vacation. And we're going to have a wonderful time —"

"Or else," Dave teased, his bushy mustache accentuating his grin.

"It's really a terrible thing." Emily shut the paper. "What must her parents be going through? I can't think of anything worse than losing a child."

"Dylan thinks we should have canceled," Cam said. Her brother, a year her junior, was spending the month at X-treme Sports Camp in the Berkshires. As soon as he'd heard about Marleigh's disappearance, he'd called Cam.

"How can you truck now? This is the biggest thing to hit Marble Bay ever. And you, like, actually talked to her."

"There was no point in canceling our vacation." Emily glanced at them again, her pretty blue eyes peering from under her blond bangs. "What could we have done? Besides, the town is completely overrun with reporters and tourists."

"You know," Dave mused, "this whole 'disappeared diva' angle is just too pat. It wouldn't surprise me if it turned out to be a publicity stunt."

"Cam is sure Marleigh was kidnap —" Cam's sharp elbow to the ribs stopped Beth midsentence.

"What makes you think that, princess?" her dad asked.

Dave Barnes was a lawyer. But not, Cam liked to point out, one of those shark types. He was seriously sensitive and often took on cases for people who couldn't afford his firm's usual fees. *Pro bono* it was called, and Cam was super-proud of him.

Except for his shirt.

He was actually wearing the Hawaiian monstrosity his office gang had given him as a vacation going-away gift. They'd meant it as a gag, Cam was sure. But here he was, wearing it.

Ordinarily, she'd never think of lying to her dad. Right now, however, she couldn't tell him the truth.

What was she supposed to say? That a skinny old white-haired guy she'd been dreaming about since childhood had suddenly appeared in Marleigh's seat and urged Cam not to go to Montana? That he'd hinted Marleigh would need her help? That he'd said something like, "She's going to be snashed." Which sounded a lot like snatched. Which, last time Cam had checked, still meant taken, grabbed, stolen, or kidnapped.

Right. That would go over as big with her folks as it had with Beth. Especially with no-nonsense Mom, whose goal in life was to produce healthy, well-balanced children.

"I don't know," Cam said, shrugging and fiddling with her baseball cap. "Nothing really. It's just a hunch, an intuition." She tried to make light of it. "You know, my famous sixth sense."

"Oh, I forgot," Beth intoned suspensefully. "She . . . sees . . . kidnapped . . . people."

"You put the 'un' in funny," Cam muttered, wishing desperately that her best friend, or someone — anyone — besides herself, had seen the bony old guy in the stands. What was Beth going to do next — remind her how she'd blown the game? One goal was all they'd needed. Instead she'd heard his scratchy voice, seen his face, and she'd frozen. Single-handedly causing Marble Bay to lose the tournament. A whole season down the drain. Because of her.

Despite Dylan's belief that they should have stayed home, Cam thought, getting out of town, not having to face her teammates, was the best thing she could have done.

Still, something about this vacation was creeping her out; something other than wondering if she'd gone around the bend; something weirder than hallucinating an aging gremlin who might or might not have predicted Marleigh's disappearance.

Usually, her family went to Hilton Head Island, South Carolina, for two weeks of golf, tennis, and tanning. But this summer they'd accepted the invitation of a grateful client of her dad's to spend time at his resort ranch in Montana. Saddlebrook, the rambling place was called, and the guy who owned it had a strange name. Sot Naht. Which Dylan, of course, had morphed into Snot Knot.

At first, Cam had been grateful to be far from Marble Bay, scene of her infamous freeze and possible mental meltdown. She'd been psyched that Beth was along. They could have fun anywhere. But since they'd arrived, she'd been feeling even more spooked than she had at the game. There was something about being here, in the wide-open spaces of Montana, that made her feel unsettled. Lonely even.

Right. Lonely, when she was around almost

everyone who totally mattered to her. Definitely, she was losing it.

She'd meant to ask her dad how he knew this Snot Knot guy. In the living room of the lodge, there was a huge portrait of a burly, well-dressed, bearded man. A man with burning black eyes who, she assumed, was Mr. Naht. She wondered what business he'd had with her dad.

"Earth to Cam. Your vote, please?" Her mom's voice interrupted her thoughts. "We've got two choices. We could go to the frontier theme park over at Crow Creek. It's supposed to be an authentic re-creation of life in the 1800s. Or, there's a fascinating conservation walk . . ."

Instantly, Cam clicked back to the reality zone. Some things never changed. Like, her mom on a mission. There had to be some edu-aspect to their vacation. It was a Barnes family requirement.

That's what she was doing — Cam wanted to remember — *she'd been smiling at the back of her mom's salon-perfect blond 'do, when the vote was taken. That's what she'd been thinking — how her mom was so flawless and predictable — when a totally random decision was made. Where to spend a few hours on vacation. A simple little decision that would change her life forever.*

CHAPTER SEVEN
CLOSE ENCOUNTER

"Welcome to Big Lie . . . I mean Big Sky."

That was the way Alex sometimes greeted tourists. In her cheesy, fringed vest, she worked the ticket booth at the east entrance to the theme park.

She checked her watch. A half hour more and she'd be off duty. Then, she'd meet up with her posse, Evan and Lucinda, and they'd hang out and goof on the crowd while scarfing junk food. The kind with names as bogus as Big Sky itself. Rank-tasting stuff like "pioneer burgers," "bunkhouse chili," "rodeo franks," and Alex's personal favorite, "buffalo chips."

"Can I get four all-day passes, please?"

Alex glanced up to see a dude with unruly dark hair,

a walrus mustache, and a bushy canopy of eyebrows overhanging small, twinkling blue eyes. The guy had a natural grin that made him seem easygoing and made her want to smile.

He nudged two fifty-dollar bills in the slot toward her. "That's good for every attraction and ride, right?"

She nodded, then couldn't help adding, "As many as you can live through, sir. It's part of our Frequent Survivor Package."

Luckily, he smiled at her — then tilted his head and shot her a curious look. She was used to that, since most of her customers were easily thrown by her hair-du-jour. But mustache man seemed neither shocked nor disapproving. It was almost as if he recognized her and was about to say, "Do I know you?"

To which Alex would have responded, "No way." This dude, in his happy tourist Hawaiian shirt that showed his sunburn line at the sleeve, was so not from around here. Then again, who was?

It was summer, Big Sky's big season. Vacationers swarmed the grounds; bought T-shirts, bolo ties, and souvenir vests; had Polaroids taken outside the "genuine" Wild West saloon or behind papier-mâché bars in the "authentic" sheriff's office, or waving from the top of the Ol' Wagon Wheel — which was Big Sky-ese for broken-down old Ferris wheel.

Making fun of tourists was easy, a cheap thrill that — okay, yeah, yeah, Alex got it — had more than a hint of envy to it. But it was like, summer vacation, whoo-hoo. Watching smiley-faced families — mom, dad, junior, and sis — romping through overpriced, phony-baloney "attractions," run by the pathetic, underpaid "townie" staff. Spew much? Alex could.

For her, "summer" and "vacation" didn't belong in the same sentence. Summer? She could work longer hours. Vacation? Alex's mom never got a day off. Dude, Sara'd be losing money this week because she had to go to the clinic.

A shadow fell over Alex's heart as she thought about the cough her mother'd had for weeks now. Maybe months. Alex didn't know how long it had been. Unsurprisingly, Sara had been secretive about it — as she was about anything that might cause her daughter to worry. She was always trying to protect her, shield her from . . . from reality, Alex guessed.

Reality: They were alone, broke, and paddling like crazy just to stay afloat. Reality: For the bonus round — Sara was sick and they couldn't afford a decent doctor, so she'd waited weeks for today's clinic appointment. "Only two weeks," her mom would say — like that was nothing.

Sara could put a positive spin on anything. Like when people called Alex "different" instead of "cute," or said she looked "interesting" instead of "pretty," her mom would beam — like it was the hugest compliment — and proudly announce, "That's Alexandra, that's my girl."

Again, Alex checked her watch. Fifteen more minutes. She wished she could call her mom right now, find out what they'd said at the clinic. No one was at her booth this second. If she'd had a cell phone, she could make the call.

Right, like that would ever happen. It was so not a mystery why seeing kids parade around the park, giggling into their StarTacs and Nokias, totally annoyed Alex. They could speed-dial their buds, who were like ten feet away, and go all "whaasssuup?"

Idiots.

Alex couldn't find out if her own mom was okay until she got off work, broke out of her cage, and used a pay phone.

She took a deep breath. Chill, girl, she told herself. You're out of here soon.

"Change of plans." Lucinda's apple-pie face suddenly filled the ticket window. It was a face that not even fifty skinny braids, two of them dyed orange, could make seem anything but innocent. "Evan says to meet him at the Wagon Wheel. Henry got sick so they sent Ev over there. We're gonna go up for free."

Alex scrunched her nose. "Up where? On the wheel? We want to do this, exactly, why?" Evan was a flake, for sure, but the Ol' Wagon Wheel, Big Sky's totally hurting, state-of-the-last-century ride? They never did that.

"It's free, that's why," Lucinda repeated. "Come on, Als. Just one ride. It'll be a blast."

One ride. A blast.

It only blasted Alex's whole universe to pieces.

Evan saw it first. Clarification: saw *her* first. On the Ol' Wagon Wheel. But in typical Evan-speak, he did the lame-joke thing.

"Hey, Alex," he called, leaning over the side of their creaky, swinging basket. "There's a girl two carts down who stole something from you."

Alex did a fast calculation and came up blank. Her money was in her jeans pocket. Her backpack was stashed in the gear house at the bottom of the Ferris wheel. She folded her arms across her chest, waiting for the punch line. "Okay, Ev, I'll play. What'd she steal? My Stratocaster, SUV, or cell phone?"

Evan pointed down. "Your face."

Alex rolled her eyes. "Don't quit your day job, Evan. Comedy Central is not scanning the globe for you," she said, rubbing a sudden rash of goose bumps on her arm.

Lucinda flipped around to check. "Get outta here! Alex," she shrieked. "He's right. She looks just like you —"

"Only cleaner," Evan teased.

"Could you be any less funny?" Alex challenged. But her stomach lurched nervously, or maybe it was just the cart swinging in a gust of wind. "Nobody looks like me," she declared, going along with the joke. Although — between the goose bumps and fluttery stomach — she was acting way cooler than she felt. Finally, she peered over the side of the cart to check it out.

A pair of tourist girls were two cars below them. One was string-bean skinny with a mop of frizzy hair. The other, about Alex's size, was wearing a baseball cap and a Gap-khaki's ad-itude. As if she felt someone staring at her, she turned abruptly and looked up at Alex. Their eyes locked. Their remarkable silver-gray eyes, stormy irises outlined in inky black. Wolf-gray, witch eyes.

Alex felt the unexpected sting of hot tears. Dizzy suddenly, vision blurred, eyes burning, she gripped the seat railing to stop herself from pitching forward.

And then she heard a yelp of distress, a gasp — as if the tourist in the baseball cap had seen her and cried, "No!" A single word, called out in surprise, wounding as a blow. Alex heard it clearly, yet knew the girl hadn't said it aloud.

And there were the goose bumps again. And a raw

emptiness in the pit of her stomach — as if she'd suddenly recognized, identified, a feeling she'd had all her life. Now it had a name. Loneliness.

Quickly, Alex turned away from the stranger and struggled to calm her pounding heart.

What was happening to her? The Ol' Wagon Wheel was just a dumb ride, one of the oldest in the park, way tamer than the Bullwhip or the Six Shooter. So why was she chilled, clammy, shaking? Why was she scared?

And why had a tourist's gaze left her light-headed, left her blinking black spots as if a flashbulb had gone off in her face?

"Is she your spitting image, or what?" Lucinda prompted.

"Oh, yeah, she's wearing my favorite color, puke pink," Alex heard herself say, sarcastically. "And I'd never leave home without my too-cool, slim-line cell phone, right, Luce? We're a perfect match."

"You are," Evan insisted.

"Not," Alex noted.

"Get out," Luce protested. "How can you say that?"

"Look at her hair," Alex grumbled. "Under that cutesy little cap, it's all wavy with, like, reddish highlights."

"Exactly like," Lucinda smirked triumphantly, "what's under the blue dye job I gave you?"

*   *   *

"Did you see her? Did you see?" Beth tugged on Cam's arm. "How freaky-deaky is that?"

"What?" Cam asked, trying to clear her head. Looking at the girl Beth was talking about had left her woozy. Her senses, at first blazingly sharp, had dulled painfully. It was as if she'd been staring directly into the sun. Her eyes were tearing. She could hardly see anything now — only shadows. "A couple of kids pointing at us?"

"No, that's not it," Beth asserted. "It's that other girl. The one not pointing."

What Cam had seen, before being temporarily blinded, was a fiery, gray-eyed girl with a shock of electric blue hair bobby-pinned at random angles to her skull. Something seemed familiar about her, Cam thought. And then, with a shudder, she thought, No!

Don't go there, girl, she told herself. Pretend, just pretend you're sane.

CHAPTER EIGHT
DIRECT CONNECT

"Cam, don't you see it?" Beth squealed. "She's like identical to you!"

"So you're saying I came two thousand miles from home to, what, find my evil twin?" Not daring to look back up at the girl in the fake-suede, fringed vest, Cam forced herself to laugh. "That wouldn't even make a bad TV movie of the week. Way to dish the compliments, Beth."

Beth was stunned. "This is no joke, Camryn. This is like the weirdest thing ever. How could you not see it? Did you suddenly go off? Like at the —"

"Soccer game? Could we please not revisit that scene?"

Reluctantly, Beth dropped it. Cam put on her sunglasses. And the two friends spent the next five minutes in an uneasy silence broken only by the rusty creaking of the Ol' Wagon Wheel.

They were both grateful when the ride ended, but Cam's relief was short-lived. As she and Beth hopped out of the cart, she saw the kids who'd been pointing — and knew they were waiting for her.

The tall boy with his fuzzy dreadlocks and the chubby girl with her Pippi-Longstocking-goes-punk braids were totally obvious in their staring. Only the blue-haired one with the fierce eyes was ignoring them. Stooped down, she was busily rummaging through her backpack.

Cam felt queasy, off balance, not really up for a meet 'n' greet — not with her eyes still burning from their midair clash, and her heart racing so fast she wasn't sure she could speak. What were the odds, she wondered desperately, of pretending not to see them and just moving on?

A deliberate tap on her arm told her, slim to none. It was the boy. "Any chance you'd take off that hat?" he blurted. "And the shades?"

And let them see her bleary eyes? "Uh —" Cam grew panicky and shot Beth a let's-make-a-quick-exit look.

But Beth stood rooted.

The girl of a thousand braids spoke up. "Don't mind

him, okay? Sometimes he slips back into his native language: rude."

In spite of herself, Cam grinned.

The girl continued, "We couldn't help noticing that you look so much like our friend here." She pointed to Alex, who was still kneeling on the ground, her back to everyone. "We thought if you took your hat off, and the sunglasses, we could see your face better."

"No," Cam blurted. "I mean, I can't. They're prescription," she lied. "I can't see a thing without them."

But Beth was all over it. "We noticed it, too," she squealed. Then to Cam's astonishment, her best bud actually tapped backpack girl on the shoulder and said, "Would you mind turning around?"

Slowly, Alex got to her feet and turned toward Cam. As they stood face-to-face, the gasps from their friends were so pronounced that people nearby turned to stare.

They were exactly the same height.

They had the same build.

Their lips were full. Their noses gently sloping but bobbed, blunt at the nostrils. Their cheekbones wide, chins strong, and slightly, rebelliously, thrust forward.

Their expressions — of shock, distress, pure panic — were mirror images.

Cam saw her own eyes reflected in her sunglasses, only it was the other girl's amazing eyes.

Alex heard a heart beating wildly, only it wasn't her own. It was the girl in the baseball cap's.

"I look nothing like her."

Cam's hand flew to her mouth, as the exact same words came blasting out of the stranger's lips.

It was too much, way too much to take in, to deal with, to believe. They couldn't possibly look so much alike, say the same thing at the same time, even sound alike. . . .

This can't be happening, Alex told herself. I'm just stressed about Mom — too little sleep, too many crazy dreams, too much work and worry. Taking a step back, she caught Tourista Number Two gaping at her. "Better take Willow out of the sun, Buffy," she told Cam, sounding moodier than she'd meant. "I think your friend is hallucinating."

"Must be contagious, some airborne virus," Cam stammered defensively, "because your friends are just as delirious." It wasn't Beth who was seeing things, she thought, it was her — first the white-haired old man at the soccer match, and now a bad-tempered double in a theme park in the middle of nowhere.

Beth was astounded. Verbal attacks? Not Cam's style.

"We have to work here," Alex countered. "What's your excuse? Was it a choice between this and the nature walk?"

How'd she know that? Cam wondered.

Nature walk? Where'd that come from? Alex asked herself.

Evan and Lucinda were stunned. Okay, Alex had a bite to her, but only when provoked. And she knew better than to go at it with a paying customer. Alex needed this job.

Lucinda inserted herself between Cam and Alex, and extended her hand. "I'm Lucinda Carmelson, he's Evan Fretts, and this is Alexandra — Alex — Fielding. We live over in Crow Creek, and like Alex said, we work right here in the park. Alex's at the ticket booth," she couldn't help adding, as if that were something to be extra proud of.

To Cam's dread, Beth took a step forward and shook Lucinda's hand. "That's so cool. I'm Beth Fish, and this is Cam, Camryn Barnes. We're from —"

That was it. Cam had had enough weirdness for one week. She grabbed Beth's ropy arm and pulled her away, blurting, "We're from . . . not around here."

"Massachusetts," Beth said.

"Well, buh-*bye*," Cam called, racing off, dragging Beth with her. Despite her best friend's startled protests, she didn't slow down until she'd found the rest room, with its hokey COWGIRLS sign, and dashed behind it.

Beth was ballistic. "What's wrong with you? You totally blew off those kids. How could you act like that?"

"Like what?" Cam said, out of breath. Hands on her

hips, she took a couple of deep sucks of air. "I'm . . . I'm just . . ." How could she explain it to Beth, who was clearly more excited than alarmed that a stranger had turned up looking eerily like Cam? How could she explain that she didn't want, couldn't take, any more spooky surprises? That seeing things others didn't see, hearing voices no one else could hear and, now, bumping into this distorted mirror image, was more than she could handle right now?

"No matter what," Beth lectured, "even if you're still bummed about the game, or freaked by the creepy vibes at Saddlebrook —"

"Beth, you have no idea what happened at the game," Cam began.

"Give me a break. This is me, Cami. And that girl with the blue-streaked hair is —"

"She's who? She's what? She's nobody!" Cam exploded.

"You!" Undeterred, Beth finished her sentence. "She's you."

Cam felt like a punctured balloon, leaking adrenaline. She had no strength left to battle her best friend. Instead, she found herself fighting back tears.

Instinctively, Beth put an arm around her. "I know this is weirding you out," she said softly. "It's tripping me, too. But don't you even want to find out who she is?"

Cam shrugged and busied herself digging for a tissue in her tote. "No," she said, blowing her nose. "I don't want to know who or what she is. I don't want to have 'mojo.' Or be different from other kids —"

"You're not," Beth gently assured her. "I mean, in lots of ways you're not."

In front of her friends, Alex forced herself to laugh. "As advertised, that was such the blast! What can we do for an encore? I vote for the buffalo chips at Chuck Wagon Charlie's. Equally vomitacious."

Usually, Alex was expert at getting her buds to change the subject. Or to do anything she wanted. Now they circled her.

"How could you let her go like that?" Evan challenged. "She's on your turf, with your face, and you let her trash-talk us and walk away? You don't got game, Alex."

"Unlike you?" Alex glared at Evan, who, at that moment, stumbled on an empty film canister some tourist had tossed away. Only his pride was bruised, however, when both girls laughed at him.

"Yo, bro, I'd work on that eye–foot coordination thing before you go disrespecting my game," Alex hooted, relieved to dodge the spotlight.

As if that would derail Lucinda. "What's going on

with you, Als?" she steamrolled on. "You've been a space cadet for the last few weeks and now this UFO thing happens and you don't even want to investigate?"

"UFO? What's that, Lucinda-speak for Unidentified Ferris wheel Omens?"

"Unexplained Face rip-Off," Evan quipped.

Alex chuckled, hoping to mask the dread she was feeling. And the opposite, but intense sense of . . . well, something like peace. Completeness.

"Look, this is bogus." Alex tried to clear her head. "I've got more important things to deal with than some Kinko's copy from Massachusetts."

"What could be more important than finding out who she is?" Lucinda demanded.

"My mother," Alex snapped. "That's a ton more important. I'm going to call her right now."

Evan stepped in front of her and gently squeezed her shoulder. "You spoke to your mom less than an hour ago. I doubt anything's changed."

He was right, of course. The minute she'd gotten off work, Alex had mad-dashed to the pay phone. Her mom, at the Laundromat, had answered right away. Between coughs, Sara had told her, no, the results weren't in. "Relax, baby, I'll see you later. Go with your friends, you deserve a little fun."

Fun, right. She'd remember to add that to her "to do" list.

Now Lucinda was in her face. "It's her eyes, Als. The girl's got the same creepy-peepers as you."

Alex refused to respond. But that didn't stop one-track Luce from hurtling on. "Don't you believe in fate? We've all got these doppelgänger things. It was fate that you just met yours —"

"Doppelgänger? Shopping at Words R Us again, Luce? Color me impressed."

That cracked Evan up, but didn't dent Lucinda's iron will. "Tease me all you want, Alexandra Nicole Fielding, but that won't change a thing. That girl is you."

"And that girl . . ." Out of the corner of her eye, Alex spotted a pale blond, sunglasses-wearing tourist. Hoping to reroute Luce, she flipped around to point her out. "Isn't that Marleigh Cooper? Maybe your favorite departed diva is hiding out in broad daylight? Come on, Luce, this is your kind of obsession. Where's that inquiring mind when we really need it?"

Swing and a miss. Lucinda and Evan whirled around, but the girl Alex had fingered was too short by half a foot to be mistaken for Marleigh.

"You're just trying to get my mind off your double." Lucinda caught on. "And it isn't gonna work."

As the trio trekked the park, Alex was able to tune her friends out. Only she couldn't find the off switch to the music playing over and over in her own head. The one that kept circling back to tourist girl.

They looked nothing alike, really. Okay, their features were similar. But New England Cam-chowder was a tidy little trendoid, complete with cell phone, a pure Banana girl. They couldn't have been more different where it counted. Plus what was up with those whammy eyes? Alex had wound up with flu symptoms just from glancing at the girl?

The girl. A little girl. Very little, very young . . .

Suddenly, Alex was overcome by a pull more powerful than her own brooding, more urgent than anything she'd ever felt before. It was as if, all at once, she knew exactly where she needed to be. And, without a "gotta go" or good-bye to her headstrong homeys, Alexandra Nicole Fielding raced toward it.

It was happening. Oh, no, not here. Not now. Not again.

Cam's eyesight got sharper as her hearing dulled.

She knew Beth was talking to her, but she couldn't make out the words.

What she saw, though she was too far away to see it

so clearly, was the iron arc of the Ferris wheel outlined against the tangerine afternoon sky.

At the top of the ride, holding tight to the safety bar in front of them, were two people, a man and a woman. Between them, glowing like a separate sun, a gleaming, dazzling, radiant jewel, was a child. A girl. A little girl. Very little, very young.

"I'll be out in a minute, okay?" Beth repeated, disappearing through the door labeled COWGIRLS.

Cam nodded, or thought she did. Then, just as it had at the soccer game, a cold sweat soaked her, an icy breeze set her shivering, the thudding of her pulse was suddenly louder than the laughter and chatter of the crowd around her.

She didn't know what was wrong. She only knew that something very, very bad was about to happen.

CHAPTER NINE
GOODNIGHT MOON

Racing through Big Sky, Cam retraced her path past snack stands and ticket booths, the Wild West saloon, the sheriff's office. Startling tourists and scattering those in her way, she ran until, finally, she arrived, perplexed and panting, back at the Ol' Wagon Wheel.

Instinctively, her head jerked up. The late afternoon sun was fading over the horizon. A full moon shone directly overhead. How extraordinary, she thought, the sun and moon visible in the same sky.

The Ferris wheel had stopped. Empty carts and those filled with people rocked gently, silhouetted in space. New passengers were being ushered onto the ride. But it was the metal basket on top, swaying at the very crest of the wheel, that captured Cam's attention.

In that cart, fifty, sixty feet above the park, exactly as she had pictured them, a family waited for the ride to begin. A young father, his smiling wife, and their baby daughter. The man had one arm wrapped tightly around his child's tiny waist. With the other, he was pointing at the early moon and whispering in his daughter's ear.

Cam saw it in impossible detail. The little girl's worried smile, her dainty hands clutching at her father's shirt.

And then she saw the bar above them, the steel rod from which the cart swung. The once sturdy pole that fixed the steel basket to the ride's frame seemed slightly lopsided. And loose. Two huge bolts usually held it to the Ferris wheel. Only one of them was left — and it looked as though it were tearing away from the shaft.

Cam squinted at the bar, zoned in as if her eyes were a telescope capable of focusing ever more precisely on the distant, dangerously loose bolt.

A jolt, one strong gust of wind, and it would come undone. The cart would be wrenched from the rod above it, tear off the ride's frame, and plummet to the ground.

Cam wanted to scream but, just as on the soccer

67

field, no sound came. She pointed, but no one was watching . . .

Except . . .

Alex's high-speed scramble had also ended at the Ol' Wagon Wheel. She stood directly opposite Cam, staring up at the very same cart, listening to the soft clanging of the loose bar and the jiggling bolt that held it.

Alex closed her eyes and the sounds became more distinct. Now she could hear a man's gentle voice telling a story — and she realized that, impossibly, the voice belonged to the man in the cart.

But how could she have heard him?

He was all the way at the top of the Ferris wheel, holding his baby daughter, reciting a line from a book, a book Sara had read over and over to Alex when she was just a child.

"Goodnight room, goodnight moon . . ."

Another voice, new, but familiar, broke Alex's concentration. "Look," it was begging. "Oh, please. Someone. Look!"

Opening her eyes, turning toward the sound, Alex caught a glimpse of herself in what, for a moment, seemed like a fun-house mirror. Someone who looked like her, if she were cheesy enough to wear a baseball cap, khaki capris, and a pink sweater set, was standing on the other side of the ride, staring, horrified, up at the same cart.

Boston's own Camryn Barnes.

Had tourist-girl heard the dad reciting, "Goodnight Moon"? Alex wondered. Could she hear the rusty creaking of the old bolt?

"Goodnight kittens, goodnight mittens . . ."

Afraid to turn away, as if her amazingly enhanced eyesight was all that held the wobbly bolt in place, Cam continued to gaze at it steadily. But she had a sense that someone had heard her unspoken plea. And, all at once, with a mingling of shock and gratitude, she knew that it was the gray-eyed girl from Crow Creek. Alex.

"Goodnight comb, goodnight brush . . ."

That ride should have been condemned years ago, Alex heard her own desperate thoughts. Why wasn't it inspected? Why wasn't it fixed? Those people —

. . . won't survive, Cam thought. I've got to help, got to do something. I can't let them die —

"Why not?" asked a deep, disturbing voice, a man's voice.

Cam shuddered. Pure dread shot through her. Shivering, she turned toward the sound and saw, in the shadow of the wheel house, a powerful, bearded man with jet-black hair and eyes that pooled dark as oil spills.

A twisted smile played across his lips as he saw her staring back at him.

She wanted to turn back to the cart, which was swaying dangerously above them, but the man's dark smile held her gaze, and then weakened and numbed her.

He could have been anyone, anyone big. He was wearing a simple shirt, blue jeans, and, despite the heat of summer, a leather jacket and thick hobnailed work boots.

Cam stood frozen, mesmerized. Energy and urgency seemed to seep out of her. She was suddenly weary, emptied of hope, hollow with despair.

In a nanosecond, a hot-dog man, pushing his cart, seemed to pop up out of nowhere. He was old, frail, with wiry silver-white hair, wearing oddly out-of-place black velvet slippers. Cam gasped. It was the old skinny guy she'd seen in the bleachers. He passed directly in front of the shadowy stranger, breaking the burly man's gaze.

Without warning, the sky darkened and a thunderous whirlwind swept through the theme park. Startled, visitors began to shout. Tickets, napkins, newspapers, trash barrels, anything that wasn't nailed down, seemed to go flying. Anxious parents gripped their children and ducked for cover.

And the cart at the top of the Ol' Wagon Wheel made a sickening sound as it swung violently.

Cam felt a tap on her shoulder. She shrieked and whirled around.

The girl with the random blue-streaked hair jumped back, yelling, "Yo, get a grip!"

"What are you doing here?" Cam gasped.

"Same thing you are," Alex heard herself say. "And we'd better do it fast."

They knew what was about to happen. Cam could see it. Alex could hear the rusty bolt squeaking as the cart carrying the unaware family was lashed to and fro by the wind.

They watched in horror as the bolt worked its way out of the rod.

"We need help," Cam shouted over the howling storm.

"Duh," Alex sneered.

"Can you see them? I mean, they look like such a nice family —"

"Grant them long life." The words flew out of Alex's mouth. She had no idea how they'd even formed in her brain, let alone exited her lips.

"Free them," Cam suddenly recited, *"of fear, pain, and strife."* She was rhyming again — just as she had at the soccer match. Bewildered, alarmed, she turned to Alex.

"Um . . . *they're young and happy, loving and good,"* Alex whispered. Her eyes were shut. Her hands balled into determined fists. *"Help us to help them as we should."*

"Tell us what to do to save . . . the mom and dad, and their young babe," Cam murmured excitedly, grasping Alex's hand.

A surge of energy tore through them.

"Babe does not rhyme with save," Alex grumbled.

"It was the best I could do," Cam argued. She panicked again, wondering what was wrong with her.

"Listen. It's working," Alex said, astonished.

Cam looked up. She couldn't hear, as Alex had, through the wailing wind, the screech of the bolt turning. But she could see it.

The loose rod began to straighten. Rust rained down as the bolt tightened.

But the family wasn't out of danger yet — not unless they could fasten the bolt, force it to stay tight in its rusty mooring. And Alex could not.

"It won't hold," she cried. "There's no nut. It needs to be soldered."

"Soldered?"

"The metal has to melt and harden —"

"Melt and harden. Er, garden, pardon . . ." Cam searched desperately for a rhyme. Then stopped abruptly as she felt the warmth of the fading day collect inside her, the sun-drenched dust burn through her shoes, her feet. Her whole body trembled and her eyes hurt, stung, blurred.

She fixed her gaze on the bolt, fighting not to blink. The steel bar turned red, and then white with heat. A wisp of smoke wound around the edge of the bolt.

Moving agonizingly slowly, the big bolt began to melt. When it was nearly liquid, when Alex's hand was gripping Cam's tight enough to stop the blood flow, another gust of wind, a swirling tornado, wrapped itself around the cart — cooling, Cam knew, the molten metal.

Alex heard it. All at once, she heard the faint hiss of fire, smelled the acrid odor of sizzling metal. By the time the dark whirlwind had passed, the cart was secure again. The family was safe.

"Goodnight stars, goodnight air, goodnight noises everywhere."

CHAPTER TEN
A LETTER FROM THE CLINIC

"What just happened?"

Beth, who'd arrived at the Ol' Wagon Wheel, was out of breath and — had Cam noticed — patience, too. "One minute we're talking, and then, snap! You're gone. No explanation, no see-ya-later. I thought it was a barf-emergency or something. I looked everywhere."

Leaning against the split-log fence that funneled passengers onto the ride, Cam could barely hear Beth. The thunderous roar in her head overshadowed the soft pelting of her friend's complaints.

"Camryn, have you totally lost it? I'm talking to you!

Why'd you run away from me and come back here?" Beth's nostrils flared, signaling borderline anger, about as close as the good-natured girl ever got.

Cam struggled to stop trembling, to quiet the clamor and come back to herself. "I'm . . . oh, man, Bethie . . . my bad."

Her calculated use of Elisabeth's childhood nickname had its desired effect: insty anger-be-gone.

"Bethie? You haven't called me that since, like, kindergarten. Wow — this is big. It has something to do with that girl, doesn't it?"

"What girl?" Cam asked quickly.

"You know, the local, that Alex kid." Beth gave an exaggerated sigh. "The one with your face, your eyes, your bod —"

"Beth, did you just see us together? Did you see what happened?!" Cam's heart leaped with hope. It was too good to be true. Had her best friend actually witnessed the stunning save? Had Beth seen what Cam and Big Sky girl had managed to pull off, with nothing but rhymes and desperate determination?!

"You mean how the two of you went mental when everyone was saying how you looked alike?"

"No, not that —"

"Then what?" Beth was clueless.

Dejected, Cam pushed off from the railing. What was she supposed to say? Did you see us doing what we couldn't possibly have done — fixing a busted, rusted old ride, rescuing a family from certain death?

It was crazy, she thought. Beth hadn't felt the irresistible force that had drawn Cam, and the stranger who looked like her, to the Ferris wheel. No one had.

And no one, not even Alex, seemed to have noticed the black-bearded guy in the shadows, whose gaze had left Cam feeling weak.

Or the other one, who'd appeared just before the windstorm, the skinny, old man . . .

No. Nuh-*uh*. Could not have happened, Cam told herself. Way too weird. If it had been real, any of it, everyone in the park would have seen it.

Okay. It's over, she decided, taking Beth's arm. Not gonna obsess about it one more second. Not gonna talk about it. Ever!

Aiding and abetting her decision, the girl, Alexandra Wilding, or Fieldhopper, or whoever she was, had vanished.

"So what happened? Why'd you take off like that?"

Cam slipped her sunglasses out of her pocket and put them on. "No bigs, Beth," she answered. "Couldn't find my shades. Figured I left them back here. And, see — I did."

*   *   *

Alex was collapsed on a bench a few yards from the Ferris wheel when Luce and Evan found her. She had no idea how long she'd been sitting there. Long enough, she guessed, to go from wondering if she'd really stopped a fatal accident from happening to trying to figure out how.

With help, was the answer. The girl, the one with the same gray eyes as her own, had something to do with it.

The million bees buzzing in her brain had quieted to a tolerable hum now. Quieted enough for her to hear Lucinda say breathlessly, "Als, hey! What are you doing back here? Five minutes ago you couldn't get away from the Ol' Wagon Wheel fast enough."

"Yeah, why'd you dump us like that?" Evan demanded. "Man, I never saw you move so fast. Now you see her, now she's a blur streaking through the tourist herd."

"You don't look all that good," Lucinda added.

"Yeah, well, your outfit rocks, too," Alex snapped. She felt wiped out. Obviously, it showed.

"Oops, I did it again, I must've lost my cell phone." Lucinda pretended to be horrified. "You know, the one that matches my trendy jeans. Sorry I'm not as cool as your new Boston buds."

"Mine?! Excuse me," Alex said, "you're the one who pushed for the Kodak moment with them."

"And you're the one who looks just like them," Luce shot back. "Like that Camryn one, anyway."

"Not," Alex barked. "You want to know why I cut out? Because I was sick of you guys riding me about looking like a tourist. Can we go now? I am so done with this day."

"You should've said something, Al. I thought something happened to your mom," Evan said, as they walked toward the gravel pit reserved for employee parking. "I thought you got, you know, like one of your 'feelings.'"

"Oh, no, did you?" Lucinda gasped. "Is your mom okay?"

Alex shuddered and rubbed her arms. "I won't know till I get home, will I?"

Okay, memo to self, she thought as they piled into Evan's rusty red pickup. I'm freaking out here. But it's because of my mom. That cough. Oh, man. It's got nothing to do with . . . what's-her-name?

The girl who's supposed to be like me.

Is . . . like me. In a way. She knew about the wheel. She was staring at the rusted bolt when I showed up. What is happening here? How could I — or, okay, even we — stop the Ferris wheel free-fall fiasco?

I don't even know why I was there. And why was

she there? And how us both being there changed something. Stopped something.

Oh, man! Like my life isn't screwy enough, now there's this? I'm just not going there. It's over.

"Maybe we should go back and find her," Evan was saying. When Alex didn't respond, he leaned over and rapped lightly on her head, "Hello, anybody home? You listening?"

"You've got a fine grasp of the obvious, Fretts," Alex answered. "I'm doing my best not to."

They were almost at her turnoff. She could see the stop sign just ahead. She unzipped her backpack and began to hunt for her keys.

Evan shook his head. "Then you'll have to do better, 'cause you've got to hear me. She didn't resemble you, Allie. She twinned you."

"What if she is?" Lucinda chimed in. "I mean, what if you were separated at birth —"

"You saying it couldn't be?" Evan narrowed his soft brown eyes.

"My mom would have told me, that's all. It's full disclosure between the two of us. Always has been."

"If I were you, I'd just have to know who she is — and why she just happened to drop into your life right now," Lucinda said.

"Good thing you're not me, Luce, because I've got a

lot of other stuff to deal with now. Stuff called real life."
They hit the hole in the road, the one Beeson kept saying
he'd fix.

Lucinda squealed as Evan's truck bounced and
clanked over the crater. "Do this one thing for me, Als,"
she said. "Let's find her. At the very least, find out when
her birthday is. If it's the same as yours, you know,
Halloween —"

"Oooooo, stop. You're spooking me," Alex cracked
sarcastically. "Can we please just drop it? First of all, I'm
so not interested in finding out anything about her. And
secondly, one day at Big Sky is usually enough for any
tourist. She's gone. Boo-hoo, I may never see my twin sister again."

The trailer was just ahead, propped up on cinder
blocks. Home sweet home.

"Oh, you will," Lucinda said. She sounded totally
sure of herself.

"And you know that, exactly how?"

"I just do," Luce announced. "You're not the only
one who gets hunches."

Her mother was home early. Their old Chevy was
parked in the rutted weeds beside the trailer. "Should we
wait?" Evan called as Alex sprinted from the pickup.

"No. Catchya later," she told them. "I'll call you."

Sara was at the kitchen table, staring out the window at the mountains. She turned as the door creaked open. And Alex was frightened by what she saw.

Her mother looked like a skeleton. White-faced, bony, the hollows around her eyes were dark with exhaustion. The skin pulled tight around her cheeks. For a minute, a split second, she reminded Alex of the nightmare man. Then her mom crumpled up a piece of paper lying on the table and grinned a big, loving, glad-to-see-you grin at Alex, and she looked like herself again.

"What's that?" Alex nodded at the paper in her mom's hand. "Another rent hike notice from Beeson?"

"Nothing for you to worry about," Sara said, her voice raw and raspy.

She was lying. Alex knew it, knew her mom better than anyone in the world. "Wouldn't be from the clinic, would it? I mean, you wouldn't mess with me, Mom, and not tell me if the news is bad?"

"How could I? Don't you always know the truth anyway? Ever since you were a little girl —"

"That letter. It's not from Beeson, is it? And the lab results. You already got them, right?"

"Oh, baby," Sara said, tears spilling from her dark eyes. "I don't know why you were given to me. I'm such a lousy . . . liar. I'd do anything to protect you, baby. Anything, if I could."

Suddenly, Alex didn't want to know the truth. "How much is he threatening to raise us today?" she asked, turning her back on her mother, walking over to the fridge and pretending to care what was inside.

Sara coughed harshly, tried to clear her throat. "Don't worry. It's not all that bad, Allie," she said, her voice muffled by the dish towel pressed to her lips.

Later that night, Alex woke to get some water. On her way to the kitchen, she passed her mother's door — an accordion-pleated piece of stiff gray vinyl that hung from an overhead track. Behind the rigid curtain, Alex heard the thick rattle and wheeze of Sara's breathing.

The crumpled letter was on the kitchen table. It had been smoothed out and lay next to her mother's empty coffee cup, as if Sara had been studying it before she went to bed.

Had it been left there for Alex to find? Did her mom want her to know what was in the note? The first thing she saw was the clinic letterhead. The next thing her eyes fell on was the word CHEMOTHERAPY.

Sara Fielding had lung cancer. Surgery was not an option, the note said, but a regimen of radiology and chemotherapy might delay the spread of the disease, possibly even put it into remission. In order to begin treatment, the letter requested that Sara fill out the following information about her health insurance.

What health insurance, Alex thought. They had none. And then it hit her full out. Lung cancer. How bad was it?

Not all that bad, her mom had said. But they'd been talking about the bogus rent increase, right? Or was it the cancer her mom had really meant? It's not all that bad, Allie. Did that mean she wasn't going to die?

Alex sat down slowly, sank into the same wobbly chair Sara had been sitting on earlier. She looked out at the mountains, which were visible even in the dark of night and resembled, Alex used to think, a dragon's back. A zigzag of peaks. Ridges silhouetted against a star-splashed, moonlit sky. It was the same full moon she'd seen that afternoon, up early and pale over the Ol' Wagon Wheel.

She thought of Cam then, of seeing the girl on the other side of the run-down ride. Alex raked her hands through her purposely stringy, blue-streaked hair. Except for their height and eyes being the same, she was nothing like the pampered princess from Massachusetts.

And didn't this prove it, Alex thought, grabbing the letter and shaking it angrily. Would little Miss Four-tickets-at-twenty-five-bucks-apiece have to worry about health insurance if anyone in her family got sick? No way.

Who cared anyhow? She wasn't part of some stupid sitcom family. It was just her and her mom now, and they'd gotten along fine, just the two of them.

Well, fine might not be the right word. They'd gotten by. They'd survived. And they were going to keep on surviving, too. Both of them. No way was Sara not gonna get the treatment she needed. Even if Alex had to work two shifts at the park or quit school and get a real job. There was no one dying around here. Least of all the one person in the world Alex trusted and loved completely.

CHAPTER ELEVEN
WHAT BETH BELIEVES

Saddlebrook Ranch was massive. "Horse Whisperer Deluxe," Beth called the huge lodge with its soaring ceilings and oversized log furniture. It had its own stables, tennis court, and even a private spring-fed swimming pond.

It also had its own strange vibe, Cam thought. A vibe that was especially strong every time she passed the portrait in the living room. Maybe it was the great height at which the painting was hung, or its subject's dark stare and cold smile, that made it seem so menacing.

"Is that the guy who owns this place?" Cam asked her dad, the day after their trip to Big Sky. She was on her way to meet Beth at the tennis court. Hugging her racket, shivering slightly, she paused before the painting.

"I don't know," Dave admitted. He was wearing boxer swim trunks as flashy as his Hawaiian shirt, and had a towel flung over his shoulder. "I never actually met the man. He's a friend of a client I defended. Hey, you're all goose bumps. What's up?" he asked, putting an arm around her shoulder.

"He looks like someone," Cam said softly, remembering the burly man in the wheel house shadows.

"Well, if he's our mysterious host," Dave chuckled, leading her toward the door, "then he *is* someone. One of your major someones. Head of some powerful corporation, mega-rich —"

I think I saw him yesterday, Cam wanted to say, but didn't. Instead she hugged her dad and, as he set off to join her mom at the pond, Cam hurried across the manicured lawn toward Beth, who was practicing serves.

She'd decided, Cam reminded herself, to drop the whole Ferris wheel episode. The eerie eavesdropper, the bony old man, and, especially, all the weird stuff that had happened with Montana-girl. It was bad enough she was freaking; she didn't need to advertise the fact to friends and family. Chalk up yesterday to a touch of flu mixed with jet lag and soccer guilt.

By the time she got to the court, she'd half convinced herself that the only connection between Saddlebrook's Major Someone and Big Sky's Mr. Weirdo was that they were both evidence of her near mental meltdown.

When Cam put her mind to something, she was usually successful. Today, her goals were to wup Beth, minimum two out of three, and to totally delete from memory everything that might, or might not, have happened yesterday. She would've been successful, too, if Beth hadn't come down with a seriously annoying stubborn streak.

Her best bud chose their tennis match to begin needling Cam about her "townie twin." At least Beth got props, Cam reluctantly admitted, for not bringing the whole deal up in front of her parents.

"You guys are the same height!" Beth insisted, as she too easily connected with a Cam-slam just inside the baseline.

"So are about half the other fourteen-year-olds around the globe," Cam contended, hitting to Beth's backhand, forcing her bud to hustle to connect — which the leggy girl did a lot more effortlessly than Cam anticipated. "Your point?" she demanded, missing Beth's return.

"My point — exactly! It's thirty–love," Beth announced the score gleefully, then served again. Smashing the ball past Cam, she added, "You've got the same body structure, too —"

"Which means nothing. Come on, Beth, can't you see how you're reaching here?" Cam retrieved the missed ball and tossed it back to Beth, who served again.

This time, Cam executed an awesome if totally accidental drop shot. Which forced Beth to breathlessly bolt to the net. Where she managed to holler between gasps, "I've never seen . . . two faces . . . so identical."

"Let it *go,* Beth," Cam warned, feeling her determination to move on crumbling. "Just drop it."

Somewhere in the back of her head, a little voice asked why she was getting so upset.

"And Cami, the eyes. She's got to be your twin."

Cam raced forward. Ignoring the voice, ignoring the ball, she met her bullheaded best bud at the net. "No, she doesn't!"

"My game!" Beth exulted, then she cleared her throat and got serious. "Okay, look. Can I ask you something? Promise you won't get mad?"

Instead of growling, "It's too late for that," Cam frowned and grumbled, "Go for it."

"Something else that's been sorta bothering me." Beth paused, embarrassed. "Remember in biology? The stuff on genetics? You know, two blue-eyed parents . . .

well, the odds are pretty slim that they'd have a kid who didn't have blue eyes, too. And yours are —"

Cam cut her off. "Go, you Marie Curie, girl-scientist! Mine are gray. But, logic takes a holiday in your hypothesis. Gray is a shade of blue."

"And your intense shade of gray — well, it's exactly the same as hers."

"Coincidence alert! That's all it means. Can we get back to our match now? I am about to fry you, Fishsticks."

Cam turned on her heels and stomped back to the service line. She smashed a wicked serve over the net.

Beth hit it back smoothly. "I think she's your twin. Your biological twin," she asserted.

"Do you even know what you're saying? There's been only one of me in my family for, like, ever! That means, what, that my parents got rid of a twin?"

"Maybe she was kidnapped," Beth offered.

"Kidnapped, right. Marleigh on the brain much?"

"It's possible," Beth insisted.

"No, it isn't. If anything like that happened, I'd know. Finding a kidnapped baby — hello, their whole lives would be all about that. You know my parents."

"But do you?" Beth challenged.

"What are you talking about?"

"Maybe you were adopted," Beth blurted out.

"Maybe you're insane!" Cam snapped.

"Cam, there *is* no other rational explanation!"

"Rational? You want rational?" Cam threw her whole body into her shot, slamming the ball so hard, her tennis racket went flying — right at Beth, who ducked just in time, then skidded and fell on the red clay court.

Cam was as shocked as Beth. Mortified, she hurtled over the net to her fallen friend. "I can't believe I just did that. I am so sorry —"

Slowly getting to her feet, Beth brushed red dust off her shins and waved Cam off. "Forget it. No damage done. Everything's all right —"

"No," Cam asserted suddenly. "Everything's not all right. Everything's wrong. Weird. Wacko." A lump formed in her throat, strangling her voice, flooding her eyes with tears. "Bethie," she whispered desperately, "I think there's something wrong with me."

They were sitting on the little bench at the side of the tennis court. Beth, visibly shaken, passed Cam the water bottle, and urged her to drink. "You're probably just dehydrated," she ventured. "I mean, there's nothing wrong with you. A spooky thing happened, that's all. Anyone would be freaked if they came face-to-face with —"

"It's not just that," Cam said reluctantly.

"Of course it is! Camryn Alicia Barnes, you are the most totally together person in the whole world. I have firsthand knowledge of that, being the best friend of the most totally —"

"I saw a face, all pasty white, a creature," Cam started.

"— together person in the . . . a creature? Oh, you mean Alex. Well, her hair was monstrous, but calling her a creature —"

"Beth, please listen," Cam urged. "In the stands. At the game. That's why I didn't make the goal. Something happened, something *is* wrong with me."

"You just choked. It's unusual for you, but it happens to the best of us. Which, may I remind you, defines you. The best of —"

"I didn't choke. I saw a face in the stands, and I just knew —"

"A bleacher-creature? That's what lost the game for us?" Beth studied Cam skeptically.

"And I knew something was about to happen. Something bad."

Beth cleared her throat. "Let's review. We're about to win the most important game of our soccer careers. You're in position to nail it for us. But instead of kicking the ball, something forces you to look up into the stands.

Where you see — what? A pasty-white, uh, creature. And so you freeze. Well, who wouldn't?" Beth dabbed gently at Cam's flushed face with a towel. "And then, I'm thinking aloud here, this thing — what? Kidnaps Marleigh? Is that about it?"

Cam didn't respond.

"Cami," Beth added, "can you hear how whack that sounds?"

"The old guy didn't kidnap Marleigh. It . . . he . . . was trying to tell me something. Warn me that she was in danger. Beth, it's not as if this hasn't happened before. I even told you about it."

Beth scrunched her forehead. "You did?"

"Back in fourth grade, remember, about the bony-faced guy from my dreams? The one who called me Apolla? My parents said it was just a bad dream —"

"I vote for that one," Beth interrupted, trying to lighten the moment.

"You didn't believe me then. You still don't." Cam shook her head. "But what about my premonitions? How sometimes I can, you know, like 'see' what's going to happen. Isn't that kind of the same thing as seeing some-one?"

Beth thought about it. "I don't know, Cami —"

"Remember last fall?"

"I was just thinking about that," Beth confessed. "You totally saved my life."

They had been on their way home from school on a street red and yellow with crunchy fallen leaves. Beth stepped off the curb. At the exact same moment, Cam saw what she could not have seen. And grabbed Beth's arm. And yanked her back.

A nanosecond later, an out-of-control car screeched around the corner and totally destroyed, ripped to pieces, the backpack Beth had dropped.

One backpack-turned-roadkill. One friend saved. Thanks to Cam's "seeing" the car seconds before it rounded the corner.

The two of them had stood there on the leaf-thick sidewalk, screaming, shaking, hugging each other, hearts thudding with panic and relief.

In a funny way, Cam felt a lot like she had that day. Now, too, she sensed that something was coming, screeching around the corner, speeding unstoppably toward her. Something even stranger than having a nightmare come true; more important than saving your best friend's life.

Her mom was gone by the time Alex woke the next morning. So was the letter from the clinic. On the kitchen table, there was a crusty sweet roll her mother had probably snagged at the diner last night, a couple of orange slices, and a note asking if Alex could please catch a ride to work with Evan or Lucinda. It was signed with five X'd kisses and a blot of purple lipstick.

Which for some dumb reason made Alex want to cry. It was all she could do not to pick up the stupid note and press the dorky imprint of her mother's lips against her own.

By the time she climbed into Evan's pickup, Alex had decided not to talk about her mom's condition. It wasn't exactly a decision. It was more like a superstition. It wouldn't be real unless she said it aloud.

They drove to Big Sky saying the usual dumb things. Evan led off with, "Another day, another dollar-fifty." But instead of getting annoyed at his lame sense of humor, Alex was grateful. She'd had enough surprises. Ordinary was fine with her today.

And ordinary it was. No emergency phone calls from her mom. No rides self-destructing. No sudden appearance of clones from across the country. Not for three whole days. Then, on Sunday, Lucinda brought Alex's midafternoon junk-food rations to the back door of the ticket booth. A bag of greasy fries and a trickle of warm cola, floating brown and flat, in a cup of chipped ice.

"Hey, what happened to that hunch of yours?" Alex

chose that exact moment to rag on Luce. "Where's the Boston bean queen, or did you have an ESP meltdown?"

Shoving the cardboard tray of gag-worthies at Alex, Lucinda grumbled, "Very funny. Oh, and by the way, thanks for being such a fabulous friend, Lucinda, and bringing me this excellent snack." Then she stalked away.

"Thanks, Luce," Alex called after her. Then she turned back to the ticket window and looked up.

Her very own face stared back at her from the other side of the booth. It was Camryn.

"I know you're busy," she blurted, "and we're on the way to the airport. I just wanted to . . ." She let it trail, shrugged, pushed a piece of paper through the window slot at Alex, and took off.

CHAPTER TWELVE
MOMS DON'T LIE

The file in her dad's study was labeled FAMILY PAPERS.

That's the one, Cam thought. If my birth certificate is anywhere in this house, it'll be in this file.

Ever since she'd gotten back to Marble Bay three days ago, she was mission-girl. Mission: idiotic, that is. As if she needed proof of what she already knew to be true, proof that would get Beth off her back.

She was Camryn Alicia Barnes, daughter of Emily and David Barnes. Born to them on October 31. Beth was wrong, wrong, wrong to suspect anything but. Like she was adopted. Right. Like she had a twin!

So whack was this "investigation," she couldn't even

admit to her parents she was doing it. So she'd waited until they were out of the house to do her sleuthing.

Already, she'd rifled through tons of old baby pictures. She hadn't come across any of her mom pregnant, but that proved exactly what? So her mom was a little camera-shy when expecting, no great revelation.

She had unearthed Dylan's "at birth" shot, taken in the hospital, a wrinkled little red-faced infant swathed in a blue baby blanket. That there wasn't a matching one of her didn't freak her. It was somewhere else, no doubt.

Now, Cam eyeballed the contents of the file. As advertised, there were several significant family documents. The deed to the house. Her parents' marriage certificate. Her granddad's will. Stocks, bonds, money stuff. And, score! A birth certificate!

As Cam started to unfold it, her cell phone rang, startling her. She nearly jumped out of her skin.

Alex, she thought. Then she realized, with a start, that she'd been expecting to hear from Montana-girl. Well, half expecting, anyway. Not really. It was just a slim possibility.

The day that the vacation ended, Cam had been seized by a wild impulse. With the excuse that she thought she'd left her baseball cap at Big Sky, she'd talked her parents into swinging by the park on the way to the airport. With the minivan purring outside the gate, she'd run up to the ticket booth and slipped a piece of paper to the girl behind the window. On it Cam had scrawled her full name, birthday, e-mail address, home phone, and even the private number of her cellular. Without explanation, she'd shoved the paper at Alex.

Alexandra. The girl with her face. The girl with whom she'd . . . she'd what? Whispered witchy rhymes, stopped an accident, saved a family?

No way, Cam reminded herself. It never happened. It was just another eerie episode in her increasingly weird life.

Still, she'd been waiting for the call. She'd compulsively kept her phone at her side and checked her e-mail messages hourly. So far, zilch.

Except now. Cam braced herself and hit the TALK button.

"Where on earth *is* Camryn Sandiego?"

So much for premonitions, Cam thought, instantly recognizing Beth's teasing voice.

Cam laughed nervously. "Channeling Bree much?" Their bud Brianna was the one always riffing on Cam's name.

"Speaking of Bree," Beth responded, "and the rest of our friends, you remember them. Names like Kristen, Sukari, Amanda? Everyone wants to know where you've been hiding. You've gone all phantom-girl since we got home. Report your location — longitude and latitude, please?"

"I'm home. Where else would I be?"

"And your pink princess phone in your bedroom is, what, too far to stretch? I just tried you on that line."

"Busted," Cam responded, feeling as if Beth could see through the phone and had caught her rifling through her parents' private papers. She went for a quip. "It's a lazy summer afternoon, and if God had wanted us to actually pick up every call, She wouldn't have invented voice mail. Or mobile phones. Anyway, so what *is* up?"

"Right back atcha, Cami. What *is* up? No one's heard from you. You're not returning messages —"

"Come on, Beth, it's just that I've been, you know, busy."

Half-truth alert. Preoccupied was more like it. Trying to find her birth certificate. Trying to pretend that Alex didn't exist . . . while hoping she'd call. Trying to remember for the police, who were interviewing everyone who'd spoken with the still-missing Marleigh Cooper, exactly what she'd seen the day of the finals. Without, of course, mentioning the nightmare man.

"Cam," Beth asked gently, "you're not still mad at me, are you?"

"For what?"

On the other end of the phone, Beth sighed. "You know."

Of course she did. For insisting that Alex, a complete stranger, had to be Cam's twin. For planting the seed of doubt in Cam's own mind. For just . . . doing what a bff — best friend forever — would do: say what was really on her mind. Tell the truth. Try to be supportive.

"Even if I was mad at you," Cam rushed to reassure Beth. "You know, where you're concerned, I'm incapable of holding a grudge —"

"Prove it. Meet me for pizza in fifteen."

"Wait!" Cam laughed. "I hear something. Aha! The sound of my stomach rumbling. Okay, Fish, give me and my humongo appetite twenty minutes, and we'll meet you at PITS."

Her spirits high, Cam hung up and finally looked at the birth certificate in her hand. It read, "Dylan Michael Barnes." Stashing it back in the file, she zipped through all the other papers. Not one of them was her birth certificate.

Pie in the Sky, aka PITS, had been a hangout for Cam and her friends since the beginning of junior high. Because the gang totaled a half dozen — besides Cam, Beth, and Brianna, there was Kristen, Sukari Woodard, and Amanda Carter — Cam's dad had tagged them the "Six Pack." The label had stuck.

"So is everyone ticked at me, or what?" Cam, sitting in a booth across from Beth, fiddled with her cell phone, making sure it was on and powered up. Just in case.

"I covered for you," Beth responded, sipping her soda. "Told them you had to do the mother–daughter bonding thing — you know, since Dylan's away for a while. They totally bought it. Everyone knows how tight you and your mom are."

Cam eyed her knowingly. "And sort of insinuated I'm not ready to face anyone since the game?"

"Posttraumatic soccer stress — totally legit," Beth admitted. "And, no, I never mentioned she-who-shall-be-nameless, your Montana mirror image. I'll leave that privilege to you." She smiled, shrugging. "They wouldn't have believed me, anyway."

"Thanks, Bethie," Cam said gratefully.

Beth shrugged and toyed with her straw. "Anyway, everyone's consumed with trying to figure out what happened to Marleigh Cooper."

"Yeah, there's a motion to rename the town 'Marleigh Bay.'" Their waiter, a tall, dark-haired boy with a cute, almost-shy smile, had arrived and inserted himself into the convo.

For some weird reason, Beth lit up. "You-so-clever,

Jason." Then she kicked Cam, a signal that Cam basically didn't get. So she ignored it and began to order. "We'll do the half veggie pie and —"

"Half extra cheese," Jason finished for her. "You've got it. Comin' right up." He left, still smiling.

"How'd he know that?"

Beth rolled her eyes. "Figure it out."

"Sorry." Cam laughed. "Flight figure-it-out is way overbooked. I'll have to put that one on standby."

"Oh, no, not again," someone at the next table groaned. He was looking at the TV perched over the counter. "Another Marleigh Cooper update. Right in the middle of the game."

"That's the mother," the girl sitting with him said. "Poor woman. Shhhh, I want to hear her."

Cam and Beth turned toward the screen, where a petite, well-dressed woman, her eyes puffy, face contorted in misery, was being besieged by reporters with microphones. Desperately wringing her hands, she was visibly shaking.

"Marleigh's mom looks positively *Scream 3*," Beth whispered. "Totally freaked out —"

"Mrs. Cooper," a reporter shouted, "any news? Can you give us . . . anything?"

"Leave her alone," someone offscreen whimpered.

The camera pulled back to reveal Tonya Gladstone, protectively pressed against Mrs. Cooper.

"Wow, it's Tonya. Talk about freaked out," Cam said. "She's a mess. She must've lost ten pounds in the week we were gone."

Marleigh's mother gratefully grasped Tonya's hand.

"Tonya, over here." A newswoman stuck a microphone into her face. "It's been over a week. Do you still feel hopeful that Marleigh will be found?"

"Of course I do," Tonya responded forcefully. "I just know my friend Marleigh is going to be okay. She has to be," she added pathetically.

"You should hear Brianna on the subject," Beth said. "Irony-alert!" She imitated Bree's breathless gush. "Guess who's become the ultimate *superstar*? Tonya! She's actually giving interviews and stuff. Oh, yeah, I almost forgot. She's had a miracle cure and thrown away her crutches. Guess they didn't look telegenic enough."

"You've got Brianna down," Cam marveled.

"Yeah, she thinks it's the mother."

"The mother what?"

"Just that there's something wacko in mom-ville. That Mom Cooper staged the whole thing —"

"Staged it? Why would she do that?" Cam rubbed her arms.

"Bree says she's supposed to be this totally control-
ling stage mother who runs every part of Marleigh's
life — and that this whole thing's a publicity stunt engineered by 'Mommy Dearest.'"

Although she had been preoccupied, there was no
escaping headline news. And Cam really had thought
she'd heard it all. The rumors. The gossip. The faux sight-
ings. The psychic predictions. The endless TV news "bulletins," and those cheesy scrawls across the bottom of the
screen. And on the radio, it was Marleigh music, 24/7 —
even though the "disappeared diva" had only released
one album. Unsurprisingly, MTV was all over it. *The
Marleigh Watch, with Carson Daly,* had eclipsed practically all programming. If this was, as some people insisted, all a publicity stunt, well . . . it was the mother of
all publicity stunts.

"Alrighty then." The lanky waiter reappeared with
their pizza — and a huge grin. "Please note," he said, setting the pie down between them, "the extra cheese half
has not run into the more contained veggie side. We
pride ourselves here on the no-spillover rule."

Cam blinked up at him, mystified. But Beth's elbow
to her ribs informed her that she was expected to say
something. "Thanks, uh, that's great, Jordan."

"English-as-a-second-language," Beth quickly explained to the boy. "She totally meant Jason."

"What's with the quick defense?" Cam hissed, when he walked away.

"Camryn. He's cute. He's trying to be funny. He's like totally crushed on you. Remembering his name would be a plus."

"Who's crushed on me?" Cam asked, surprised, checking out the gregarious, gangly boy. "I mean, do I even know him?"

Beth rolled her eyes again. "His name's Jason Weissman. He's a senior. He asks me about you every time I see him."

"You're kidding —"

"So not," Beth said, gingerly cutting a slice of the extra cheese for herself. "Anyway, polling the Six-Pack: Kris agrees with Brianna that Marleigh's mom's a suspect. Sukari is thumbs-up on the publicity stunt. 'It's all about the Benjamins,' is how she put it. But she doesn't think Mrs. Cooper's in on it. And Amanda, well, she's like me, just worried about Marleigh."

"Put me on that list, too," Cam mused. "No one's said anything about the whacked-out fan thing?"

"Did you?" Beth asked. "I mean, when you talked to the police?"

"I completely forgot it," Cam admitted.

"Me, too," Beth consoled her. "They haven't been playing that angle up on the news."

"Oh, wow, you know what else I zoned on — at the game, when Marleigh was all, 'It's so tragic.' At first I thought she was talking about Tonya's sprained ankle. But Marleigh seemed to think something else was wrong with Tonya —"

"She's not doing too well. Understandably," Beth said, glancing up at the television screen. "Hold up. Marleigh's mom's on again."

Cam turned back to the update.

"If anyone knows where my baby is, please just bring her back safely. Marleigh, if you're watching, I love you, honey. I miss you." Mrs. Cooper tried to say more, but couldn't. Unable to keep from crying, she hid her face in her hands.

Feeling a little teary-eyed herself, Cam remembered her own mom's reaction to Marleigh's disappearance. "I can't think of anything worse than losing a child," Emily had said.

How could Cam ever suspect that her devoted, conscientious, tenderhearted mom could be dishonest enough to keep secrets from her — secrets about her birth, her twin, her very identity.

The newsbreak was over. To the delight of the man in the next booth, the ball game came on again.

"So what were you doing this morning?" Beth asked casually.

"Nothing much," Cam responded, stuffing her mouth with pizza to keep from blurting out: Just sneaking behind my parents' backs, trying to find out if I was adopted, and whether my mom just forgot to tell me that I'm not really hers.

Beth chomped off a piece of crust. "Who knows," she said philosophically. "Maybe Brianna's right about Mrs. Cooper —"

Cam's black-rimmed gray eyes flashed. "No," she said. "Parents don't do that to their children. A real mother would never be that devious. Moms don't lie."

CHAPTER THIRTEEN
INSTANT MESSAGES

"I'm afraid it's too late."

For a second, Alex didn't know whether it was Mrs. Bass, the librarian, she'd heard or her own thoughts.

"Too late?" she echoed stupidly. "No, it can't be." Sure her mom was sick, very sick. But if they could get her another doctor, a better doctor, someone who knew more about lung cancer . . .

Doris Bass flipped open the cover of *Myths and Magic of the Ancient World* and showed Alex the stamped due date. "Look, here. It was supposed to be back in May. Today is July 12."

"I know. I'm sorry. Can I use the computer, Mrs. Bass?"

"You mean, while I calculate your fine?" The librarian tried to look severe, but didn't quite pull it off. "Of course I might go easy on you if you give me a good explanation for why you kept the book so long. I think I'd like to hear that you truly enjoyed it, that you're fascinated by mythology, that it changed your life."

"All three," Alex blurted. "Is it okay if I use the computer to send an e-mail?"

The librarian sighed and pushed back her chair. "How's your mom doing?" she asked, leading Alex to the computer desk.

"Not great." Now why had she said that? Did the whole world have to know? Right now, there was just one person she wanted to tell, one person who might be able to help. Correction: *Had* to help.

"I heard," Mrs. Bass said sadly, adding, "Do you have the e-mail address?"

Alex pulled the note from her pocket and unfolded it. "It's this girl from Massachusetts." She was still holding the grubby piece of paper.

"Give Sara my love. Tell her I'll stop by the hospital on Sunday," the librarian said, leaving Alex to the library's computer.

Alex slid into the chair as Mrs. Bass returned to her desk. She typed in Cam's e-mail address. Then she paused.

What message? What was she going to say? Hey, remember me? SOS. My mom is dying.

Why was she doing this, anyway? She didn't *really* know the tourist girl. It wasn't like they were friends. They'd just . . .

They'd just showed up at the same place at the same time.

They'd just magically repaired a broken ride with their eyes, minds, and desperate determination. And some whack rhymes that came out of nowhere.

Who knew what else they might be able to do together?

Alex's hands were shaking. Was she totally flipped? What did she think, that Camryn same-birthday Barnes would hop the next broomstick to Crow Creek? That they'd stand at Sara's bedside and repair Alex's mom the way they'd fixed a broken Ferris wheel bar? *If* they'd fixed the bar. Which could so not have happened.

Money. Alex tried to clear her head. That's what this was about. If they'd plunked down a hundred dollars for a fun day at the faux frontier, obviously the Barnes brood had cash to burn. And Alex wanted it. Sara needed it. They had to get a better doctor, move Sara to a bigger hospital, do something!

With two fingers, she banged out a message.

Hi. It's me, Alex Fielding, your "twin" from Big Sky. Only kidding. The thing is I need this gigundo favor. My mom is really sick. If you're interested, call me. Fast!

She tapped out her phone number, hit SEND, leaned back, and had an instant shame attack. What kind of bonehead blabbed her private business to a stranger, posted a personal 911 on the Internet? Ugh. She should have signed it Cyber-chump. Shoulders slumped, head in her hands, Alex sat there for a couple of minutes, overwhelmed by embarrassment and regret.

Then, just as she pushed back her chair, the computer made a chiming noise and the words INSTANT MESSAGE! flashed across the screen.

Hey, it's Cam. I can't believe it. I was just thinking of you!

Alex's heart leaped with excitement. An IM from Cam! Quickly, she responded,

This is almost as weird as what happened at the Ol' Wagon Wheel! You know, us being there at the same time.

Totally, came the answer, a second later. *Sorry about your mom. Don't think I'm crazy, but does she have gray eyes?*

Brown, Alex typed. *My mom's got brown eyes — and no medical coverage. That's why I was wondering . . .*

Her fingers slipped from the keyboard. Suddenly,

she was seized by a stomach pain that made her curl over and moan. Her hands went clammy. Her face felt wet. Emptied of hope, her chest felt suddenly hollow — and then an icy grief filled it.

"Alexandra?" Mrs. Bass rushed over. "What is it? What's wrong?"

"My mom," Alex gasped, "I've got to get to the hospital. Right now."

Sara was alive. Just barely.

Alex rushed into the room, almost colliding with an old, white-haired doctor who was hurrying out. There was a crackle of sparks between them as his lab coat brushed her arm.

She raced past the curtained beds of strangers to the end of the ward. A nurse sat at her mother's bedside, moistening Sara's lips with an ice cube.

"What happened?" Alex asked her.

"We've been trying to reach you," the woman said. With a tart clunk, she dropped the ice back into a metal bowl of melting cubes, and stood abruptly. "She's very weak. I'll page the doctor on duty. He'll explain."

"Wasn't that him?" Alex asked, but without answering, the nurse bolted into the hall.

"Alex?" Her mother's eyes were slits, as if she hadn't

the strength to fully lift her lids. "Baby, I'm so glad you got here." Sara's bony hand, pale and red-knuckled, reached for her. "I'm sorry, Alex. Please forgive me."

"For what? Mom, what happened? Is the chemo making you sick again?"

"I tried." Sara grasped Alex's hand. Her touch was dry and crinkly. "You're the most wonderful thing that ever happened to me, baby, and I tried to keep my promise. I tried with all my might, Alex, to be a good protector, to keep you safe."

"I'm safe, Mommy," Alex whispered. "Really, I'm okay. It's you we've got to take care of."

With effort, Sara shook her head. "Listen to him, Alex. He looks odd — scary sometimes, but he's good."

"Miss Fielding?" Alex turned to the doctor striding toward them. He wasn't looking at her. He was flipping through the pages of a medical chart.

It wasn't the same doctor she'd nearly crashed into, the one who needed static guard on his coat. This one was much younger. He had bright red hair and thick glasses.

Was this who her mom had meant? He didn't look all that odd and, certainly, not scary. More like a dork, a geek, a Waldo in a lab coat.

"Are you the daughter?" he asked.

Alex nodded, wishing the guy would look up.

"I understand the hospital's been trying to reach you."

"I stopped at the library," Alex said. Her anger at his casual attitude was instantly tempered with guilt.

"Yes, well," he said, finally facing her. "Er, how old are you?"

She knew better than to say fourteen. "Eighteen," she lied, hoping her mom wouldn't contradict her.

"It's her liver —" the redheaded doctor said.

"Her lungs, you mean?"

"The cancer, Miss Fielding, has metastasized. It's spread to other organs. Primarily her liver. I'm afraid —" He glanced at Sara, who seemed to be sleeping now. "Let's step outside."

Carefully, Alex released her mother's hand, setting it down gently on the hospital blanket. She followed the doctor out into the corridor, which was where he told her that Sara would not last the night.

CHAPTER FOURTEEN
A FAMILY SECRET

Even though a few things weren't adding up, Cam was not caving. Not to Beth, or to the tiny nagging in her own brain. Because, hello, there had to be some rational explanation for what she hadn't found in the FAMILY PAPERS file in her dad's office. Or any other files she'd looked at. Or among the hundreds of family photos she'd eyeballed.

It's probably like that forest-for-the-trees thing, she thought. When you're drowning in details, looking for little things, you always miss something. In this case, something as obvious as proof of her birth.

Still, she couldn't help running through the checklist in her head. No pictures from her mom's pregnancy. No birth certificate — except Dylan's. For whom there was also a newborn picture. And the photo with the tiny footprint.

And all that meant exactly what? Hardly a 180 of all she knew to be true.

And now there's Alex. Who looks like her. With whom she might have done some surreal thing at the Ferris wheel. Who, magically, had been on-line the exact same moment she'd chosen to check her e-mail. With whom she'd just IM'ed — until the moment, that is, that Alex had stopped suddenly.

For some reason, that disconnect had prompted Cam to just do it. Go for the obvious. Talk to her parents.

Maybe, she thought, coming down the steps from her bedroom to the den, it was because of what Alex had said. That her mom, her brown-eyed mom, was really sick and didn't have medical coverage. Alex was clearly desperate, and even though they probably weren't really related, Cam felt bad for her.

So, maybe, right after she cleared up the little matter of her birth — hello! — she'd tell her parents about the coincidence of meeting Alex. And ask if they could help in some way.

As Cam hit the bottom step, she stopped abruptly, gripped by a sudden attack of the "what ifs."

What if . . . her parents didn't react as she expected them to?

What if . . . they didn't throw their heads back and laugh at her outrageous question?

What if . . . there really *was* some deep dark family secret she didn't know?

That last "what if" made Cam laugh. She could just hear her parents going, "Oh, right, we forgot to tell you, you're not our real child. And yeah, you did come with a twin, only we didn't take that one. Now, could you go do the dishes?"

Ridiculous much?

Cam grinned. Of course her mom would say, "Oh, Cami, sweetheart, you couldn't possibly have thought that."

And her dad's teasing rejoinder would be something like, "If you believe that, wait, I'd like to introduce you to Mr. S. Claus, who's got some presents for you."

Then they'd probably march her up to the attic and present some box she hadn't noticed. Some box marked THE BIRTH OF CAMRYN: SUPERSTAR! Or something that tipped the Velveeta-meter in pure, processed cheesiness. And they'd all have this giant laugh about it afterward.

Convinced now, Cam strode down the corridor toward the family room, where her parents were watching TV. Correction: where her dad was on the couch, channel surfing and flipping through a client's file.

And her mom was curled up in the armchair, reading a book.

Cam paused, looking from one to the other. Her dad's wrinkled forehead, his stubbly chin, walrus mustache, her mom's cornflower-blue eyes, her curtain of blond bangs. Seeing their faces was as natural to her as breathing.

"Hey, look who's here." Her dad shot her a huge smile. "Off the phone *and* off-line already? That's got to be some kind of record."

"She just happens to have a lot of friends. Stop teasing her," Emily said.

Dave patted the couch. "Come join us, we're trying to find something besides the Marleigh Cooper story on TV, but we're not having much luck. The only bit of 'news' is that our own Marble Bay Music & More store is offering a substantial reward for anyone with information. Who knows? Maybe we'll get lucky and there'll be a break in the case."

Cam inched into the room. Her eye fell on a family photo. Like a zillion others scattered around the house, it was a shot of the four of them from one of their vacations. All were holding tennis racquets. Cam shifted uncomfortably.

Emily looked at her expectantly. "What's up, sweetie pie?"

"I was sorta coming down to see you guys," Cam

stammered. What was up with the nerves-relapse? "I have something weird. I mean totally weird to ask you guys."

Concern drifted across her dad's face, but he said nothing.

Cam's heart began to pound. "It's really, really important." Why had she tacked that on?

But when her dad said, "I have a feeling I know what it's about," Cam had to laugh.

"I don't think so, Daddy."

"It's a family question, isn't it?" Dave sounded pretty sure of himself.

Cam was taken aback. "How'd you know?"

Emily remarked, "Think you're the only one in the family with 'sixth sense'? Where do you think you got it from? Your dad's pretty perceptive."

Cam's jaw fell open. Is it remotely possible they know? How could they? And then she realized — professional snoop that she so *wasn't,* she'd probably left some telltale signs of her search around. Probably they figured she'd been looking for something. But, could they really know for what?

Dave closed his eyes and put his finger to his temple, doing a really bad imitation of a psychic. "You want to know about Dylan," he declared.

"And," Emily broke in, "what exactly is going on

with his room? Did we really send him away for a month just so we could take down all his posters, change his wallpaper, and toss out his old furniture?"

Cam couldn't believe what she was hearing. Just at the moment she felt this huge wave of relief, and thought that she was totally in sync with her 'rents, off they went in another direction entirely.

"He might act shocked when he gets home," Emily was warming to the topic of Dylan's room, "but I know my son. Within a week, he'll love it. And sweetie, if you want, after we're done with his, we can start thinking about redecorating yours, too. Maybe get rid of that extra bed in your room. Beth hardly sleeps over anymore — usually, it's the whole bunch of you in the basement."

Cam's stomach started to churn. Didn't she say her question was important? And changing the wallpaper in Dylan's room was what her mom thought was on her mind. She knows her son, Cam thought, but she doesn't know me at all.

"It's not about Dylan. Or his room. Or my room," she said heatedly. "It's something . . . else."

Both her parents were now looking at her with anticipation.

"Was I . . ." she started.

At that instant, Dave caught her eye, and Cam suddenly knew. Her mom had been blathering about home decor, but joking aside, her dad knew something else was up with her.

"Now I feel stupid for even asking this. . . ."

Emily broke into a grin. "As a famous newsperson once said, 'There are no stupid questions. Only stupid answers.'"

"Was I adopted?"

There, she'd said it. Her words hung in the air, three little orphans, floating above them, with nothing to anchor them.

Emily Barnes turned white.

David Barnes's jaw dropped.

Neither said a word. The only sound in the room was the thud her mom's book made after it slid off her lap and hit the hardwood floor. It wasn't until Cam's eyes fell on the cover that she lost it.

Over the image of identical infant twins facing each other in the womb, was the book's title: *I Know This Much Is True*.

At that moment, Cam knew this: Her whole life had been one big lie.

CHAPTER FIFTEEN
SAYING GOOD-BYE

Alex was numb.

Lucinda ran around the front of Evan's truck to open the door for her. Evan sprinted over to help her down.

It was weird to be wearing a dress, she thought, taking Evan's hand and getting out of the pickup.

The ground beneath her new shoes was dry. It felt solid as stone. She didn't see how they were going to dig through it. Then she looked up and saw that they already had.

There, in the rock-hard, red earth, a neat hole yawned. Next to it was her mother.

The coffin Alex had ordered looked every bit as cheap as it was, she thought. But its cargo was precious. Priceless.

"See," Luce whispered, squeezing Alex's other hand encouragingly. "There are lots of folks here."

There were, Alex saw, as she moved toward the grave site. Many more than she'd expected. People who'd worked with her mom at the laundry and the diner had showed up. Even though, Alex guessed, they'd be losing a chunk of money for taking the time off.

Mrs. Bass, the librarian, was there. And Mrs. Medgers, her English teacher. And Andy Yatz and a couple of other kids from school, which sort of surprised her.

Even Hardy Beeson had made it to the funeral. Ugh. She'd counted on having some time before the king of the tin slumlords found out that her mom was . . . gone.

No such luck.

There were even strangers there. Well, people Alex didn't recognize, anyway. And one stranger who she did. The white-haired doctor with the cattle-prod arm had showed up. He looked out of place in his black velvet vest and weird sandals. Still it was nice of him to come.

The service was brief. After the shabby, raw-pine coffin was lowered, Alex tossed the rose Evan had given her into the grave. Then she quickly turned away. The cemetery men were waiting with their shovels. She didn't want to see them begin their work.

As she stood off under a shady tree, people kept coming up to her. She nodded at most of them. Andy Yatz gave her a bouquet of scruffy flowers he'd probably snagged from someone's garden. Still, she appreciated it. It gave her something to do with her hands.

"We'll all miss her," Mrs. Bass said, reaching out to stroke Alex's hair.

Alex ducked. She couldn't help it, and was grateful that Mrs. Bass didn't seem to take it personally.

"I'll stop by later with a casserole. You've got to eat," the librarian said.

Alex said, "Thank you." Thank you was what she kept on saying. It was all she could think of. She mumbled, "Thank you," and shook hands, and kept nodding as if she actually knew what people were saying to her, as if she really cared.

"Well, we'll be talkin' soon," Hardy Beeson promised. "You know your mama, rest her soul, she owed me a pretty penny."

Finally, after everyone had filed past and wished her well and said what a good person Sara had been, Alex noticed the doctor in his odd black outfit, still standing at the grave.

She wished he'd go away. She'd wanted to say a private good-bye to her mom after the cemetery crew finished.

She could hear Lucinda and Evan. They were waiting near the pickup, talking with some of the kids from Big Creek Regional.

Alex was torn between walking the yard or so to the graveside, where the man in black velvet was standing, or just racing back to Ev's truck and leaving the cemetery fast.

She could always come back later, she decided. She could come back tonight. Alone.

Actually, you can't, the doctor said. *It wouldn't be safe. Not alone.*

But how could she have heard him? He wasn't anywhere near her.

Come over here. We need to talk.

Alex had been numb all day. Cold as stone, hard as the cemetery earth. Now feeling rushed through her, loud and lonely, like wind roaring through a cave. She began to shake.

Suddenly, she was standing beside him. How had she gotten to the graveside?

You'll be all right, he said, touching her shoulders. And, miraculously, she was.

Her trembling subsided. The howling grew still. The frozen block of ice that, just days ago, had been her heart, began to thaw. She could feel herself warming, relaxing. "You're the one from the hospital, right? The doctor I bumped into coming out of the ward?"

"I just wanted to thank Sara," the old man said.

"Thank her?" Alex asked.

"'Doesn't matter." He brushed away her question with a wave of his gloved hand. "Alexandra . . . that's what she called you, isn't it? Alexandra, I have something for you. Something from your mother. She gave it to you many years ago. It's time you had it back."

Alex ran a hand through her unruly blue-streaked auburn hair. "You knew my mom?" she asked, her melting heart aching at the thought of Sara young, Sara alive.

"I did. A more beautiful creature there never was. A proper babe. With eyes like . . ." The doctor seemed to be looking for a word to describe her mom's eyes. A delighted smile burst across his crinkly old face. "Well, with creepy-peepers like yours," he announced.

"Mom, a babe? Creepy-peepers?" Alex almost laughed. "Her eyes were brown," she pointed out.

"Gifted eyes, dark-rimmed and gray," the old doctor reminisced.

"When did you know her?" she asked doubtfully.

"Know her?" He snapped out of his reverie. "Oh, Sara, you mean. We met fourteen years ago."

Was I born then, she wanted to ask. Did you know

me, too? But he went on, "She was so strong, Sara. And she had the knack, the know-how. I thought she'd be perfect."

Sighing sadly, he reached into his vest pocket and took out a small silk-covered box. He stared at it lovingly, caressed it briefly with his palm, then pressed it into Alex's hands.

The silk case felt warm. "Should I open it now?" she asked. Her throat had thickened, her eyes stung with tears.

"Whenever," the old man said, giggling suddenly. "Whoops, here comes your posse. I'm out of here. Catchya later, Als."

Cam didn't remember bolting from the den, just the thwack of her flip-flops as she'd bounded up the stairs. Now, seconds after asking her parents a question she'd never even considered before their vacation, she was facedown on her bed, trying to calm her trembling body.

Their shocked silence told her everything. A line from a song went through her head, "Ain't it funny how you're walkin' through life, and it turns on a dime . . ."

Turning on a dime. What a dumb expression.

Downstairs, she could hear her parents. Not what they were saying, but the weepy sound of her mother's sobs crashing against the deep, distressed timbre of her dad's responses. Emily and Dave Barnes rarely argued, at least not in front of their kids. And Cam — who'd just found out she was not their kid — did not want to hear it. She jumped off the bed, plunked down hard on the swivel chair at her desk, and grabbed her headphones. With one swift motion, she jerked them over her ears, flipped on her stereo, and turned the volume up to eardrum-shattering.

The album inside the boom box rocked, but was no match for the wild cacophony playing inside her head. She grabbed for her phone. Alex! I've got to call Alex! What . . . no!! I mean Beth. I have to tell her. . . .

Her dad had gently tugged off the headphones.

"Yes. The answer to your question is yes."

Her mom went to shut off the stereo.

Cam's back was to them. And that's the way it would stay.

Ignoring them, she focused on the wall in front of her. Her bulletin board. Photos of her friends smiled back at her. Beth, Kris, Bree — the four of them eating ice cream, making funny faces at the camera. The picture of her on the soccer field with Marleigh Cooper and Tonya. Dylan strumming his guitar, trying to be cool, but not carrying it off. Scott Marino, her eighth-grade crush. What had she ever seen in him?

"Cami, please. Turn around. We need to talk."

"I have nothing to say to you," Cam responded, her voice flat. "Please leave. I have stuff to do."

"But we have something to tell you." Her dad's voice was soft, assured.

Cam crossed her arms. She resolved not to turn around. Because if she did, if she looked at her dad, she'd lose it. "I don't want to hear it. Your silence spoke volumes."

Now Dave's hand was on her shoulder, squeezing it gently. "Cami, I want you to turn around and face us. Maybe we were wrong not to tell you before. . . ."

"Wrong? *Maybe?!*" In a flash, Cam whirled her chair around. "You lied to me! My whole life! How could you do that?!"

Her mom burst into tears. "It's not like that. We never meant to lie to you."

A huge lump formed in Cam's throat. Still she managed. "Omission," she said, her voice breaking. "That's the word, isn't it? Lying by omission. Not saying something — not telling what you know — just because no one ever asked you. It's still a lie."

"You're our baby. . . ." Emily sobbed.

"I don't even know who you are." Cam's lip trembled. And then her tears came.

CHAPTER SIXTEEN
THE NECKLACE

Lucinda put an arm around Alex's shoulder. "Are you okay?"

Alex didn't know. One minute she'd been at her mom's grave talking to the strange old doctor; the next, she was sitting in the cab of Evan's pickup, between her two best friends.

She glanced past Lucinda, at the cemetery. The old guy was gone.

"Were you saying good-bye to your mom alone?" Evan asked delicately.

"No, I was talking to —" But they must have seen him, she thought, stopping midsentence. The encounter had been strange, the guy kind of spacey, but she hadn't just imagined their conversation.

Alex looked down at her hands. They were clutching *something*. Cautiously, she opened her fingers and saw the faded pink silk case that proved he'd been real.

"I'm totally wiped," she told Evan and Luce, clamping her hands shut again. "I feel like . . . like I got sunstroke or something."

"Hey, what's that?" Nothing got past Lucinda. She'd caught sight of the box.

"I don't know. Something from my mom," Alex murmured.

"Like what? Let's see," Luce urged.

Cautiously, Alex opened the pale silk case. Supine on red satin, glinting in the sunlight pouring through the windshield, was a necklace, a thin gold chain that held a gleaming half-moon charm.

Alex felt weak at the sight of it. At the scent of it, too. Impossibly, the gift called to mind snow and pine musk, a stinging, woodsy aroma that was bracing, familiar, and disturbing.

"Wow, that is so cool," Lucinda said, carefully taking the necklace from Alex's shaking fingers. "Looks like real gold."

"What is it?" Evan asked.

"The man in the moon, I guess," Alex said. "A half-moon with, like, a face or something."

"Whatever happened to that skull necklace I gave you?" Evan wanted to know.

"Duh," Lucinda said. "Was that back in third or fourth grade, I forget. That black lipstick, tongue rings, and skull accessories thing is so played."

"I've still got it," Alex assured him distractedly. "Somewhere."

"Did your mom used to wear this?" Luce studied the half-moon, perplexed. "Could I have seen it on her?"

"No." Alex shook her head, then added, "I know, it's like I've seen it, too. Somewhere."

"Here, turn around," Luce said. "I'll put it on you."

Alex turned to face Evan as Lucinda held up the necklace. "Whoa, it's way too small," Luce said. "This must be from when she was a baby."

Evan cleared his throat. "So, uh, what're you gonna do now, Als? I mean, you can't live out at the trailer all alone."

It was a good question, one she'd put off thinking about. Taking back the necklace, Alex shrugged. "I won't be able to, not for long anyway. Beeson's gonna hassle me for money and I just spent about every cent we had on the funeral. Besides, the doctor at the hospital may have believed I was eighteen, but everyone in this town knows better."

"You can live with us," Lucinda volunteered.

"Sure, all your folks need is another mouth to feed." Forcing a smile, she squeezed Luce's hand. "Like, with your sister's kids staying there, ten isn't enough, right?"

"They're crazy about you, Alex," Lucinda insisted. "I mean, if my pops had a job, they wouldn't wait a hot second to take you in."

"My mama's drinking again," Evan confessed. He said it like it was a big joke, but Alex smelled the burnt hurt rise off him. "Otherwise, I'd ask you to stay at our place. But she's too . . . you know how she gets . . . unpredictable."

She thanked them, told them how totally the best they were, and asked them to just drop her at home. She felt like being alone, she said.

Not alone. It wouldn't be safe, the old doctor had warned before. Now, sitting up, wide awake, feeling Luce's arm around her, seeing Evan's big hand on the pickup's clutch, she heard him again: *Good idea. Hit that hovel, that old tin rattrap. I'll meet you there.*

He came out of the trailer as Alex was waving goodbye. Evan's truck was halfway to the blacktop by then.

She guessed she should have been freaked by his sudden appearance, but she wasn't. She was out of edgy energy, felt lulled by the woodland scent of him. "What were you doing in there, Doc?" she asked.

"Doc," he said, savoring the word. "I like that. Packing up your stuff," he answered. "You don't want to stay here anymore, do you?"

It struck her that she didn't. She didn't even want to go inside. But where else could she go? "My mom told me about you," she said, sitting down on the trailer's sunbaked step.

"Really?" He seemed pleased. "What did she say?"

"Um, well," Alex began, "she said I should listen to you."

"Good. Go on," he encouraged her, grinning.

"Well, and that you looked odd and scary sometimes, but that you were good."

The old guy cleared his throat and rubbed his nappy white head. "Right she was. Been called worse." He sat down next to Alex on the metal step.

"You're not really a doctor, are you?" she asked, surprising herself.

"I'm actually very skilled at the healing arts," he protested. "Of course, you could be, too, with just a little practice." He gestured at the green thicket surrounding the trailer. "Get to know your herbs and flowers," he advised. "Study your crystals and stones. You've already got a flair for incantation."

He saw her puzzlement. "Incantation. It's a kind of a rhyming, spellbinding wish or hope."

A rhyme? A spellbinding wish or hope? Is that why she'd broken into rhyme along with Cam, that day at the Ol' Wagon Wheel? She was about to ask, but Doc was still talking.

"For instance." His eyes fastened on hers. Alex was surprised to feel a strange pull, almost a connection between his watery blue eyes and her own suddenly sleepy gray ones.

"If you believed in magic and wanted to enchant someone, cast a spell, make them eager to do your bidding," she heard Doc say, "you might recite this incantation. 'Oh, sun' — for you, I think moon would work," he decided. "'Oh, moon that brings us light and cheer, shine through me now to banish fear; free —' and here, you'd put in the person's name, like Alex," he explained. "'Free young Alex from doubt and blame, win her trust and lift her shame.'"

Alex felt almost lightheaded, as though a burden had been lifted from her, a massive stone rolled off her chest.

"Of course," the old doctor continued, "to properly use that spell, you'll want a sprig or two of burdock or chamomile or lemon balm — all easily found — or a bit of quartz crystal." He reached into his vest pocket and pulled out a faceted pink stone. "Like this," Doc said, "to rub between your fingers."

Alex opened her hand and he placed the delicate, rosy object gently in the center of her palm. The stone felt cool at first, but as her fingers closed over it, she could feel it heat up. "Oh, moon that brings us light and cheer," she began to recite.

"Whoops, whoa, hold on there," Doc said, retrieving the crystal. "I said it works if you believe in magic. Then there's always this one: 'For good alone I ask of you, help this child speak fair and true, let her say or do or be a fearless friend who'll trust in me. . . .'"

Alex could barely open her eyes.

"Never mind," he laughed. "All in good time. Oh, but please call me Doc. I really like the sound of it. Now let's talk about you. What are we going to do with you? You can't stay here."

"In the trailer? Why not?" Alex asked.

"No, in this place, this . . . *Montana*. There's been a sighting. What I mean to say, Artemis —er, Alexandra," he corrected himself, "is that it's not safe."

Alex remembered the mythology book. "Artemis, lady of the hunt, protector of children and wild things, the moon goddess."

"Ah," Doc crooned, "I nearly forgot, I brought you a new chain. A longer one."

He held out his gloved hand. In it, amidst a crumble of herbs and bright-colored stones, was a delicate gold chain, three times longer than the original had been. She took it and, like the crystal and the pale pink box, it seemed to grow warm in her palm. "What's the green stuff?" she asked, inhaling the fragrant flakes that clung to the shiny new necklace.

"*Scutellaria lateriflora*," he replied. "Commonly called 'skullcap.' Excellent for relaxing before an important occasion."

"Before?" It seemed to Alex that the most important occasion, the most significant event of her young life, her mother's funeral, had just ended.

She wanted to explain that to the old man, but a bone-weariness crept up on her. The very blood in her veins seemed to thicken and slow. "What am I going to do?" she asked, feeling sluggish and dreamy. "Where am I going to go?"

He took her hands and pulled her gently to her feet. "I know just the place," she heard him say.

CHAPTER SEVENTEEN
THE TRUTH

"What else didn't you tell me?"

Cam had been sitting at her desk, refusing to move, she didn't know for how long. A little while ago, her distraught mom had left the room. Now, she watched as her dad, pacing, rubbing his hands together, explained everything. Attempted to, that is.

She could hear him, but processing his words, understanding them, that was something else. Something that was going to take a long, long time.

Time: The one thing that girl Alex didn't have. The girl — maybe her sister! Whose mother was dying. And what if Alex's mother was really Cam's mother, too?

So while Cam heard David Barnes tell her all this stuff . . .

About how much he and Emily had wanted a child, but hadn't been able to conceive.

. . . She kept interrupting him. "What about the other one?"

About how they'd adopted her — a beautiful, wondrous, amazing daughter, a baby he knew was special from the start.

. . . "Why didn't you take her, too?"

About how the day after Cam had arrived, Emily had found out she was pregnant.

. . . "Is it because her mom was too poor to keep both of us? So they gave one away?"

About how uncannily alike Cam and Dylan had looked, how they'd just moved to this new neighborhood and everyone assumed the babies were biological siblings.

. . . "You don't understand. She needs me! The nightmare man told me — that day at the soccer game. Now I know who he meant. He must've meant Alex. Alex needs me!"

About how hurt she might have been, how she might have thought she was less loved, less truly part of the family — if as a child, she'd been told that she was adopted, but Dylan was their biological child.

"I met her, I met her in Montana. We're the same. I mean, not the same, but we both . . . feel things. I can't explain it."

About how the longer they'd put it off, the harder it got to bring up the subject. So they just never had.

"We have to help her! We have to find her. I'm the only one who can help her."

In their hearts, they never felt Cam wasn't their own child —

Now Cam was shouting, "Why aren't you listening to me, Daddy! She needs money! Her mom is dying. And her mom might be my —"

Exasperated, Dave steadied her. "Cami, you don't have a twin sister. I think I'd know."

"Oh, please!" Cam twisted her sun necklace tightly around her forefinger. Without planning to, she suddenly yanked it hard, breaking the chain. The second it hit the floor, Cam kicked it across the room. "I always thought you gave me that necklace when I was born. Now I know even that was a lie. You didn't know me when I was born."

Dave had watched the necklace skid across the floor, but made no move to retrieve it. "You were wearing it when you came to us —" he started to explain, but Cam cut him off.

"How could you start lying all over again? Dad . . . I mean, Dave" — she threw that in, knowing it was a knife in his heart — "you have to stop lying and give it up. Give it all up."

Behind his round glasses, tears bubbled in his eyes. Instantly, Cam felt nauseous. Good going, girl — today, you made both your parents cry. Do you get extra credit for that?

"Cam, we couldn't love you any more, no matter what. And I promise I am not lying. I don't know anything about a twin."

"I met her!" Cam bolted out of her chair. "I just told you, why aren't you listening to me?"

Her dad encircled Cam in his arms and pressed her to his chest. Reflexively, she closed her eyes and inhaled. The sweet smell of his aftershave, what she always thought of as "the dad smell," filled her senses. In spite of her resistance, some of the tension eased out of her.

"That's good," Dave said. "Take a deep breath and calm down." Then he listened as Cam told him again about meeting Alex. How the stranger had been identical to her. How their eyes were the same. She told him everything, except the most important thing of all — that, together, they'd done something impossible.

He heard every word, and kept insisting that he believed her. He promised to look into it, but he swore, he didn't know anything about another baby.

Cam pulled away from him and stuck her chin out.

"If you won't tell me, then give me the name of the agency. I'll find out on my own."

Dave hesitated.

"You owe me that much, at least."

"It was a private adoption, Cam."

"But someone had to set it up. I know you." Cam pointed at him. "You're a lawyer. You would never do anything illegal. You went through some agency."

"There was no agency."

"Then let me see my birth certificate. It'll say if there was more than one baby. I saw that on TV. It'll say 'multiple birth.'"

Now her father trembled. It scared her. He sat down and took her hands. "There was no birth certificate, Cami. Not an authentic one."

Cam's jaw fell open. She felt as if a speeding soccer ball had just connected with her gut. How could this be?

"Cam," her dad began.

But she held up her hand, to stop whatever it was he was going to say.

One level down, the front doorbell chimed. So loudly, the sound reverberated through Cam's entire body.

"What's wrong, Cami?" her dad asked. "It's just the door."

She heard her own voice, sure and commanding. "I know who it is."

CHAPTER EIGHTEEN
THE BEWILDERED VISITOR

"Alex?" Cam called, before the door was fully opened.

"Cam?" Alex stood on the front porch, dazed.

"What are you doing here?" they asked each other.

Alex looked back at the driveway, but Doc was gone. "I'm not sure," she said.

"Come in," Cam answered at the same time. Seizing Alex's hand, which was tightly gripping a little duffel bag, Cam pulled the bewildered girl inside.

A crackling charge passed between them. They both yelped. It was as if their hands touching, palm to palm, had formed a weird circuit, a connection through which an electric energy surged.

It was like, Alex thought, the static rush she'd felt the first time she'd brushed against Doc's arm. Static squared.

Cam's senses seemed suddenly sharpened. What, a moment before, had been a low murmur of voices from the hallway, became now clear and vivid words. "Oh, Dave, how can this be happening?" she heard.

"Who's that?" Alex asked. "Why is she crying?"

Startled, Cam said, "My mom. Sort of." Her dad must have rushed down the stairs after her — now, he and her mom were in the hallway. Luckily, they couldn't see the front door from where they were standing. "It's just a friend," Cam called in her parents' direction, and then quickly led the confused visitor upstairs.

Alex's gray eyes widened as she took in Cam's room — the spaciousness, soft carpeting, and light; the riot of colors created by tacked-up posters, old greeting cards, snapshots, sports memorabilia, cartoons, articles, and fashion photos torn from magazines. It was a room so big it held two beds, twin beds. One of them was nearly buried under mounds of clothes, books, magazines, and CDs.

Cam rushed into Alex's line of sight, apologetically plucking up wrinkled T-shirts, jeans, and pairs of neon-bright shorts off the pile. "I haven't had time —"

"To put everything away," Alex finished the sentence. "I know."

"It's my Montana stuff." Flustered, Cam raced into the bathroom that linked her room with Dylan's and dumped the handful of clothes into the hamper. "But you could care less, right?"

"Good guess," Alex agreed, setting down her duffel bag. "Your room is nearly as big as our whole house —"

"Your whole trailer?" Cam asked, returning.

Alex sat down on the edge of the still-messy bed, the few square inches not filled with Cami-stuff, and studied her look-alike curiously. "I said house. I meant trailer. So, can you, like, read minds? I mean, can you hear people thinking?"

"Not usually," Cam answered cautiously. "Why, can you?"

"Sometimes," Alex said. "In school I heard what this kid Andy Yatz was thinking about me."

"I can see stuff," Cam volunteered impulsively. "I mean, I can picture stuff happening, but like really clearly, before it happens. And during the soccer finals, this girl from the other team, Lindsay, said I blinded her. And I think I did."

"Can you make things move?" Alex asked.

"Nuh-uh. Can you?" Cam's heart was pounding. She almost felt like crying and laughing at the same time. How crazy was it that she could talk to someone she barely knew, about stuff she'd kept hidden practically forever? And that this stranger, this girl she'd only met a week ago, acted like it was all normal.

"You mean besides turning Ferris wheel bolts hundreds of feet above me?" This was definitely bizarre, Alex decided. Okay, they looked alike, they were weird alike, but basically she was spewing secrets to a stranger. She threw herself back onto the pile of vacation gear. "I don't know," she lied.

"You can, right? You just don't want me to think you're a freak —"

Alex's mouth fell open. "Well, how freaky is that remark? Pretty good for someone who can't read minds. And, by the way, how did you melt those bolts?"

"I don't know." Cam sat on her own bed, opposite Alex, who was staring up at the ceiling. "A lot of spooky stuff's been going on lately —"

"Yeah, right. Tell me about it," Alex said sarcastically. Then, after picking at a cuticle, she asked as casually as she could, "Know any incantations?"

"Incan-whatses?"

"You know, like magical wishes or hopes that rhyme." She was almost immediately sorry she'd said it. She must've sounded like a total goon-ball, she thought, some wand-waving, barefoot airhead. Well, at least she'd stopped short of chatting about crystals and herbs.

Was that what she'd done — subconsciously — at

the Ferris wheel? What they both had done? Unexpectedly, Cam said softly, "I'm not sure. I might."

"You might what? Know how to cast a spell?"

"When we were at the Ol' Wagon Wheel," Cam answered, "something weird happened."

"Yo, dude, understatement of the universe," Alex cracked.

Cam smiled. "You know any?" she asked. "Spells, incantations?"

"Sure." Alex said it like a joke. "I know two of them. You need a magic crystal for one."

She was waiting for Cam to groan, or cackle, or just tell her she was nuts. Instead, Marble Bay Missy said, "Can you recite it?"

"Uh . . . sure," Alex said. "But you've got to turn your back because it's way powerful. It might make you do something you'd regret." To her surprise, Cam obediently turned and faced the wall.

"Okay, here goes." Alex closed her eyes and recalled Doc's words. It pleased her that she remembered most of them. Most, but not all. Then, the most amazing thing happened. Cam, with her back still toward Alex, finished it.

"Whoa, what've you got hidden in your dingy duds?" she asked, reaching behind her, into Cam's Montana mess. "And by the way, in the spooky-stuff-going-on sweepstakes, you're not even in the game. Trust me, your life can't get more offtrack than mine," she said, sitting up and drawing out the plastic CD case that had been layered in Cam's mile-high pile of stuff.

"Oh, man. I'm sorry. Your mom, is she okay?" Cam asked.

"She died. Wednesday," Alex responded brusquely. She didn't want to think about it, much less talk about it. Plus, she'd already caught the quick, pained surprise in Cam's eyes and preferred to take a Pasadena on the pity.

Ducking her head, Alex forced herself to focus on the CD in her hand. It was Marleigh Cooper's debut album. Marleigh Cooper, the diva who'd disappeared in . . .

Marble Bay, Massachusetts.

So that's where I am, she realized.

Of course. It was where Camryn Barnes lived. The girl had scribbled her address on the note she'd handed Alex. It just hadn't registered before.

"She died the day after you e-mailed me?" Cam asked, sounding confused. "The very next day?"

Alex's shoulders slumped. "Technically," she said, tossing the CD onto the bed. "It was about three in the morning. The funeral was Friday. It was okay. A lot more people showed up than I expected —"

"Alex," Cam gasped. "That can't be. Today is Friday, it's Friday night. You couldn't have gotten here so fast, unless you flew the Concorde — and I don't think they go between here and Montana."

Alex sighed, "This old guy, Doc, got me here. I must've fallen asleep or something. I don't know *how* he got me here, only that he did. He said he knew just the place for me. Way wrong," she added, indicating Cam's humongous, oh-so-cool room. "Like I belong here? So not. He must have been mental."

"But what about your dad? Does he know —"

"He's dead," Alex said sharply, and stood up. To get away from Cam's startled gaze, to outpace her own panic, she began to roam around the room.

"Why are you so . . ." Touchy, Cam was going to ask but didn't. She stopped because the answer to her question was suddenly apparent. All at once, her eyesight sharpened, and all she could hear was her own thudding pulse. She "saw" a trailer in the woods — the same trailer she'd pictured when Alex said 'our house' — and a pretty but worn-out woman coughing. Around the woman was a circle of light that was rapidly changing colors.

An aura, Cam thought, wondering how she suddenly knew the word. And then how she knew that the woman's name was Sara, and that she was Alex's mother.

And maybe her own.

Then the vision shattered.

CHAPTER NINETEEN
THE CHARRED PICTURE

"You were thinking about . . . your mom just now, weren't you?" Cam asked breathlessly.

Tears flashed in Alex's eyes. She wiped them angrily on the sleeve of her black dress. "That falls under the heading 'So Not Your Business,'" she shot back. "Anyway, you don't read minds, remember?"

Behind the bitter words, Cam sensed a painful sadness. "I'm so totally sorry about your mom," she said.

"Why? She's not your mom," Alex snapped, doing what had become automatic for her lately — turning fear, sorrow, and now grief, into anger.

How would you know? Cam wanted to blurt. But obviously, Alex was hurting. And Cam's head ached. The vision, or whatever it had been, had left her eyes burning. "Right." She backed off. "So, anyway, what was she like? I mean, only if you want to talk about it," she said. "She was pretty, wasn't she?"

"She was pretty tough," Alex answered, checking out the photos pinned to Cam's walls. "Strong, funny, generous. She's the best. I mean, she was . . ." Alex trailed off. She didn't want to talk about her mom — especially not to Cam. Suddenly her attention was drawn to one of Cam's pictures, and she blurted, "Hey, it's that girl from the news." It was a dumb thing to say, but it beat bawling again. "It's her and Marleigh Cooper — and you."

Cam glanced at the photo Alex was studying. "The one you're pointing to, that's Tonya Gladstone. How'd you know?" she asked. "Oh, I guess you saw her on TV."

"Well, duh, dude! We do have TV, even in the wilds of Montana," Alex shot back. "And newspapers and magazines. And some of us can even read them."

Cam winced. The girl, her own sister maybe, her twin, was such an irri-tator-tot, annoyingly moody. Her sarcasm was grating. Then Cam felt a stab of guilt — Alex's mother had just died, the girl was in a strange place, not even knowing how she got here. Cam guessed Alex was entitled to act any way she wanted, probably.

But still, Cam didn't want to have to watch every word she said. After all, it wasn't as if her own past few hours had been trauma-free. She'd just found out she was adopted! And you didn't see her all moody. Whatever.

Cam's cell phone rang. Saved by the bell, she thought.

"We even have mobile phones," Alex added, disdainfully watching Cam pull the cellular out of her tote bag. "But only for the overprivileged, tech-toy trendoids."

Her fingers wrapped around the phone, Cam hesitated. "I don't have to answer it," she felt compelled to say.

"Why? Because the alien from outer Montana just landed? Oh, please. Be my guest."

"Thanks for your permission." Cam grumbled, flipping open her phone.

It was Beth. "Cami. Omigosh. It's awful. You won't believe what happened —"

"Right back atcha. I've got enough awful of my own to deal with," Cam muttered, half-hoping Alex was listening. Listening? The girl could hear thoughts, she reminded herself.

"Seriously. They found a body," Beth blurted. "A blond girl, about Marleigh's age —"

A shiver rippled through Cam. She glanced up to see Alex staring at her. "Where?" Alex mouthed.

"Where did they find her? I mean, the body?" Cam asked Beth.

"In Boston. Near one of the colleges, I heard. Do

you think it's true? They're not saying, but . . . oh, please, Cam, get one of your feelings now — and tell me it's not Marleigh."

"Tell her it's not and just hang up," Alex ordered, turning back to the photo of Cam, Marleigh, and Tonya.

"Gotta go. Can't deal right now," Cam said, clicking off the phone, furious. Who was this girl after all to start bossing her around?

She glared at Alex's back for a second, then focused her angry gaze on the Marleigh and Tonya pic. With a stunning hiss, the metal tacks holding the photograph began to fume, glow, and melt.

Alex jumped back just as the charred picture slid off the wall. "Talk about toast!" Startled and impressed, she broke into a grin. "Dude, you're smokin'! What are you, a one-trick pony? I mean, how do you *do* that?"

"I don't know," Cam admitted, shaking. Torn between shock and delight, she felt almost giddy. "Why do you have to get up in my face like that?"

"*Your* face?" Suddenly, Alex was laughing. "Yo, it's my face, too," she said.

Which, a second later, cracked Cam up. Snorting and choking, she rushed to the bathroom to get a tissue. "Is this the weirdest thing that ever happened to you?" she called to Alex. "Please say yes."

It felt so good to laugh. It felt silly and careless and

unavoidable. "Why, you really think we look alike?" Alex asked mischievously.

Cam couldn't answer. Dissolved in squalls of laughter, she could barely speak. She was still convulsed when the door burst open and her parents barged into her room.

"Are you all right?" Dave demanded anxiously. "Camryn, what happened to you? What did you do to your hair?"

He was looking at Alex.

A peal of hysterical laughter drew his attention to the bathroom. "I'm over here," Cam cackled, waving from the doorway.

Dave gasped. The look on his face set Alex off again. Her shoulders shook as she tried desperately not to break up.

Emily's scream helped. It snapped Alex right out of her giggles.

"What is going on here?" the frightened woman demanded in a voice high-pitched with alarm.

Cam walked over to Alex, took her hand, and raised it triumphantly. "This is my sister," she said. "My twin sister. Obviously."

It was nearly midnight when Dave ran out of questions. "Okay, let's review," he began to summarize in his lawyerly way. "You kids met in Montana, at the park —"

"Hey, *now* I remember you," Alex put in. "I was in the ticket booth. I sold you four all-days. And you looked at me kind of strange, like you knew me."

"Small wonder," Dave muttered.

"You saw her and you didn't say anything to me?" Emily accused. She looked like she'd been hit by a truck — a truck hauling strawberries. Her pale skin was mottled with crimson blotches, and her eyes and nose were red-rimmed from crying.

"It didn't seem important at the time."

He turned back to Alex. "You just lost your mom. Your dad died some years ago. You're in high school, and there's nothing and no one in Montana you care about."

"Correction," Cam interrupted. "There are her friends, Lucinda and Evan."

"No adults," Dave amended. "A strange man who knew your mom brought you here. But you've got no money and no return ticket. And you had no idea you had a sister."

"A twin," Cam said.

"Possible twin," Emily corrected.

"Until you met Cam at Big Sky. Is that about it?"

Alex nodded. She looked very tired, Emily thought. With those pale cheekbones and wonderful gray eyes just like Cam's, and that wild, blue-streaked hair, she reminded Emily of a young wolf, one of the grieving cubs she'd seen on the nature special about Yellowstone Park. That forlorn cub, too, had lost its mother.

The girl was exhausted, Emily realized. And so was Camryn. And so, to tell the truth, was she. "Dave," she said quietly. "She's willing to take a DNA test, to find out if they're . . . related. Why don't we all get some sleep? You can phone Biogentech first thing tomorrow morning and make an appointment. And then we'll know whether they're really . . ." She forced herself to say it. "Twins."

CHAPTER TWENTY
THE UPPER PENINSULA

Coventry Island was one of a dozen low-lying, heavily wooded islands off Lake Superior's Wisconsin shore. Chill gales blew off the water, cooling the densely forested land even in summer.

At first, Karsh thought that was why he was shivering — the sea breeze on his papery skin and, of course, exhaustion.

What had he been thinking, transporting himself and the grieving Artemis across a continent? He ached all over now.

Someone was following him. Karsh quieted his busy mind to better hear the footsteps, to catch the scent of his pursuer.

He was tempted to transform himself into a hawk again, or a deer, some fleet-footed or high-flying woodland creature. But he was too tired.

The effort of shape-shifting, of enchanting himself to carry the girl two thousand miles, had worn him down. His sinewy arms, which only hours ago had been enormous wings, still stung with windburn. His face felt raw. And his back, the back that had cradled the sleeping child, would it ever be free of pain again?

Enough. The icy vibration along his spine should have warned him immediately. Now he heard the muted sound of pine needles being crushed, the crunching cadence of someone walking behind him.

Karsh reached casually into his leather pouch and searched among his herb vials for the large crystal rock. Finding the sparkling stone with his fingers, he clutched it in his palm, made a fist, and murmured the incantation.

Then, tired as he'd felt a moment before, he released the crystal, whirled around, and grabbed the terrified warlock by the throat.

A child, a skinny boy of seventeen or eighteen, wriggled in his grasp.

"Lord Thantos would like to know where his nieces are," the frightened youth stammered.

"What are you, a sensitive? A fledgling? An adept?

Surely, not a tracker. I see by your hobnailed boots you're a follower of that demented wizard."

In Karsh's grasp, the boy was turning colors, his pale face passing from mottled red and blue to ashy gray. And already Karsh's arm had begun to tremble. He could not hold the lackey much longer.

"Oh, for pity's sake, drop the idiot!" Ileana's voice exploded behind him. "And by the way, old trickster, I'd like an answer to his question."

"How could you? Without consulting me?" Tramping through the pine forest with Karsh at her sandaled heels, Ileana was hurt and furious.

He had never seen the self-absorbed young witch so shaken.

He'd have liked to tell her how urgent it was to get the girl out of Montana. How near Thantos had been to both of Aron's daughters at the theme park. How arrogant the burly wizard had grown — surfacing without a disguise, showing his true, black-bearded face in public.

But, Karsh dared not mention his encounter with the mighty warlock. Not now, while Ileana ranted at him. Not even to explain how he'd stepped between the monster and his prey, broken Thantos's hold on Apolla, and almost turned the renegade tracker into a clam.

Ah, but then he'd have to confess that the moment he'd begun the clam spell, he'd felt the fire on his forehead and heard Thantos murmuring the incantation that would have turned him, the venerable Karsh, to ashes.

So, they'd had to call it a draw. The brazen bully, saying that he meant just to see the girls together, to measure their strength, which he appraised as excellent — had fled the park. And Karsh had stayed, disguised as a wiener vendor, to help the twins if they needed his services. Which, quite amazingly, they had not!

He'd taught them well, in their dream states, to accept their legacy and invoke the secrets of their craft.

He'd trained Apolla how to hone her sight, to see not just far but deep; to dazzle, stun, and burn if need be — as her namesake, the sun prince Apollo, would.

To Artemis, he'd revealed how to listen, like the huntress she'd been named for, to sounds others would never know.

He'd whispered incantations, herbal potions, the healing uses of flowers, stones, and crystals. So much he'd poured into their young ears — and watched, in awe today, as they'd displayed their gifts, for the first time, as they were meant to be used — for the good of others.

It took all of Karsh's energy to keep calm in the face of Ileana's frenzy. To appear calm, at any rate, while hauling her bulky baggage through the woods. As usual, her suitcase was jammed with more gear than anyone else would need for a two-day trip.

"You were away," he pointed out, huffing and puffing to catch up with her, "vacationing at a spa."

"It was not a spa." Ileana stopped abruptly, stomped her foot, and smacked her thigh with the magazine she was carrying. The glossy publication cracked like a riding crop. "It was a spell-casting seminar."

"In California?" Noting her radiant tan and the sassy new outfit she wore under her flaring robe, Karsh raised his singed eyebrows — the mark his encounter with Thantos left him — skeptically.

"Los Angeles has some of the most adept spell-casters and hex-masters in the world," Ileana countered. "I met dozens of fabulous sensitives, fledglings, protectors, guardians, and trackers —"

She really was very young, Karsh thought, surprised as ever to feel a rush of affection for the vain little creature.

"Witches and warlocks from every walk of life," Ileana went on hotly. "You can't even imagine who was there."

"Not unless I use the telepathy I perfected before you were born," the tired tracker muttered. Louder, he asked, "Could it have been Brice Stanley? Prince of the Hollywood —" What did they call him, the stateside magazines and tabloids? The cookie? The sponge cake? The eye candy? Karsh recalled.

"Show-off." Ileana glared at him.

She was right, Karsh thought. Did he have to demonstrate his superior gifts when she was already in a tizzy? A moment later, when he experienced the tingling in his hands and feet, and saw the webbing grow between his fingers, he realized how truly irked she was.

"Stop it this instant, Ileana!" he croaked, feeling his throat swell. "Turn me into a frog and I'll have you up on charges. Wrongful use of power, transformation of an elder —" He was shocked at her audacity, but proud, too. He hadn't realized how very powerful she was becoming.

"I learned it yesterday," Ileana boasted. "Just thought I'd give it a try."

Stepping out of the forest, Karsh saw more evidence of her growing talent. The herb garden was flourishing. The plants looked twice as tall as they had just days ago. He couldn't help being impressed. "I'm sorry you're displeased with my decision," he said gently. "You know I rarely interfere. But I believed Artemis to be in danger —"

"And you think she's safe now?" Ileana fumed. "If Thantos found one of them, there would be danger. If he captures them together, there's only doom."

"She had no one to turn to. Nowhere else to go —"

"Doom!" Ileana thundered. "For all concerned, may I

remind you. I am their appointed guardian. Who do you think is going to take the fall if they're found? Me, you shape-shifting old trickster. Little *moi*."

"Just say it was my doing," Karsh blithely advised.

"Don't think I won't!" With that, the rage seemed to sigh out of the still-youthful witch. Her slender shoulders slumped. Her beautiful face turned grave. For a moment, she looked like what she was, Karsh thought tenderly. An inexperienced enchantress, still terrified of making a mistake.

"Exalted one," he said gently, "they've already met. I've seen them together. Their power is formidable. Twice as strong as either one's alone. They'll need it to ward off their enemies. To stay safe, they'll need to work together."

"Do they know about Lord Thantos?"

"Not yet —"

"Good," Ileana decided. "You'll say nothing to them. They're too young to know they're the targets of such fury."

"Yes, good witch."

"Goddess," Ileana snapped, taking her suitcase from Karsh. "I had no idea Brice Stanley was one of us," she said, sounding like a petulant child. "He looks so . . . human."

No sense in reminding her, Karsh thought, that the young movie star was human, that they were all human.

Ordinary human beings with extraordinary gifts and skills — such as levitation, shape-shifting, spell-casting, prophecy, mind reading, and the like. No matter what level they were at — sensitives, fledglings, adepts, protectors, guardians, and trackers — they were, in the end, just human beings with great gifts for healing and helping others.

Of course, in other times and places, they'd been called shamans, sibyls, seers and soothsayers, oracles, fortune-tellers, tricksters, even magicians. They'd existed in every culture through history.

In this day and age, they were called witches. Witches and warlocks.

Some, like Ileana, the wily Thantos, of course the twins, had inherited their abilities from their parents. Others had not been so lucky. They — himself among them, Karsh reflected, with a satisfied smile — had worked long and hard to achieve excellence.

Most people had the basics — keen senses, good hearts, teachable minds — but some had been born into families that recognized and nurtured their gifts; others, Samaritans, who longed to be of service to the race, discovered their abilities themselves.

Sara had been one of the best, until the foul sickness took her. She'd given up so much — home, husband, and health — to protect the fledgling witch Artemis.

David Barnes was another.

But Ileana was in no mood for a lesson in witchology. Nor was he prepared to give one. His aching back needed intense therapy, as did both his arms. Unless he got to Coventry Clinic soon and saw a specialist, he'd be useless to them all — Artemis, Apolla, and Ileana.

CHAPTER TWENTY-ONE
A BODY IN BOSTON

Before she opened her eyes, Alex knew she wasn't home. The sturdy mattress beneath her felt nothing like the sagging slab of foam rubber on which she'd slept for years. There was the crinkle of fresh linens against her cheek instead of the thin, pilled sheen of threadbare sheets. Even the light was different. Too bright, hot-red behind her closed lids. And the voice, "Bulletin, bulletin. Breaking news on Marleigh —" was not her mom's.

Neither was it Cam's, the stranger with the greeting-card-perfect life, who might just turn out to be her sister.

Without stirring, Alex listened.

"Why are you whispering, Cam-o-rama?" the unfamiliar voice asked.

The question was clear but distant. There was a metallic echo, a hint of static, behind it. The static, not the voice, reminded Alex of how Cam's pal, Beth, had sounded yesterday on the phone.

She realized she was hearing someone — not Beth, not Cam — speaking on the telephone. This pleased and puzzled her because she'd never been able to hear phone voices before, never clearly from across a room.

Ever since she'd arrived, ever since Camryn Barnes had taken her hand, Alex's senses had become sharper, especially her hearing.

She'd known Cam's parents were coming upstairs last night. Muffled by her own laughter and by Cam's, she'd heard a soft, scared voice say, "Dave, we have to find out," and then, footsteps on the carpeted stairs. They'd come busting in, the pretty but puffy-eyed blond woman and her lawyer husband, a second later.

Emily and Dave. They'd turned out to be okay. They even smelled good. Emily was all marshmallows and gardenias — soft, sweet, powdery, but with a perfumed sting. Dave's scent was . . . friendly, Alex thought. Green and earthy, like a new garden. They were both pretty nice, just nervous and confused.

No more than she was, Alex had to admit, and about mostly the same stuff. Like what she was doing at their house, how she'd gotten there, and why. In spite of their confusion, they'd invited her to stay, for as long as she needed to.

She opened her eyes and squinted cautiously into the sunlight. Against the morning brightness, a shadow girl with sleep-tossed hair was hunched in front of the window, whispering into the phone.

"It's okay. I'm up," Alex said as the shadow took on her own features and became Camryn Barnes.

"Oh, you're awake," Cam said. Clamping her hand over the mouthpiece, she added, "It's my friend Brianna — with a Marleigh update."

Alex heard the echoey voice. "Cam, hello? Who are you talking to?"

Cam sidestepped Bree's question. "What's the bulletin?"

"Okay. You're gonna flip. Guess what some poor kid at B.U. found?"

"B.U.?" Alex asked.

"Boston University?" Cam said into the phone. "Now what could it be? Not the unidentified body of a blond girl about Marleigh's age and size."

"You already knew! Either you got one of your feelings, or someone told you. It better be a mojo thing, 'cause no way was I scooped on this," Bree complained on the other end. "Who told you?"

"Beth," Cam answered. "Last night."

"No way. Beth Fish, the person least likely to know outstanding dish? Go ahead, just stab me — wait, wait! Turn on the radio, Cami-sole. They're talking about it now."

Alex rolled her eyes. "It's not Marleigh," she said, switching on the radio between the beds.

"It's probably not her," Cam said into the phone.

"What's up with that?" her friend responded. "You having one of your mojo moments, Camay?"

"With a vengeance," Cam answered, just as the announcer said that the body had been identified, but police would not release the victim's name, pending notification of her family. "According to police, only one thing is certain," he intoned. "The deceased girl is not Marleigh Cooper."

Cam heaved a sigh of relief. Then she eyed Alex as she teased Bree. "You want a real bulletin? I've got one that'll make your hard-to-hold hair stand straight up."

"Spill!" Bree ordered.

In one sweeping motion, Alex snatched the phone away from Cam. "Catchya later, Bree-ski," Alex said, hanging up.

"Why'd you do that?" Cam demanded.

"Because you were about to tell her about me, and I'm nobody's scoop," Alex retorted, wandering over to Cam's photo wall and studying the pictures again. "So what do you think happened to Marleigh?" she asked, abruptly changing the subject. "I mean, people don't just disappear. Except for me, of course." She gave a guilty groan. "Ugh, Lucinda and Evan'll be ballistic about my just taking off. I didn't even say good-bye."

"How come?" Cam asked.

Alex ran a hand through her stringy dyed hair. Her natural roots were showing, brown, with coppery highlights. Auburn hair. Exactly like Cam's. "Everything just happened so fast," she said.

"Do you want to call them?" Cam offered. "You can use my phone."

Alex thought about it.

"I know, I know," Cam said. "You want privacy. I'm going to take a shower."

As soon as the bathroom door closed, Alex punched in Lucinda's number. A very sleepy girl answered on the fifth ring. One of Luce's nieces, she guessed. "Ooops, my bad, what time is it?"

"I don't know," the child answered. "Everybody's still sleeping but me."

She'd forgotten the time difference. She was about to apologize again and hang up, when suddenly Lucinda was on the line. "Alex?"

"Luce! How'd you know it was me?" Was she carrying some random germ, a mind-reading virus, that infected everyone she came in contact with, Alex wondered.

"I can't believe it!" Lucinda was shrieking. "It's really you! Every time the phone rings, I keep hoping it'll be you. Als, what happened? Where've you been? Is Evan with you? We were at the trailer till like way after dark, waiting for you. I had to come home. Is he still there?"

"I don't know," Alex said. The sound of Luce's voice nearly brought her to tears. "I mean, I'm not there. At the trailer —"

"Good thing," Lucinda said, "'cause that loser landlord of yours showed up."

"Hardy Beeson?"

"Als, I never knew how scary he was. Man, the minute he started pounding on the door, me and Evan were like, uh-oh, what's up with this? It was like some hot wind went blasting through the place. We were just burning up, broke out in a sweat and everything. Hot under the collar is one thing, but this guy was literally steaming. You could see waves of heat coming off him. And he *really* wanted to know where you were. When we said we didn't know, I mean, like after about the hundredth time, he stomped his foot, and Alex, it went right through the floor! Those dumb boots of his, they, like, burned right through the floor of the trailer."

"Beeson?" Alex asked, shocked. "Impossible."

"It was him, all right. He was still wearing his tacky funeral getup," Lucinda insisted.

"The man's certified, Luce. But strong enough to stomp his foot through the floor? No way."

"Okay, okay. But we both saw it, me and Evan. Anyway, if he tries to scam more rent money from you, tell him you know who pounded the hole in the kitchen floor."

"Luce," Alex said softly, "I might not be going back to the trailer for a while. I'm . . . pretty far away."

"What, like did you go up to the creek or something?"

The creek. Crow Creek. Ten miles from home, Luce meant, where Alex's mom used to take them wading, where she'd taught them to skip stones when they were little. It hurt to remember. Alex took a deep breath. "I'm in Marble Bay, Massachusetts," she said.

"Right, Dorothy, and I'm in Oz. What are you doing there, anyway, looking for Marleigh Cooper?"

"No. I'm . . . Luce, remember that tourist girl at the park? The one you thought looked just like me? I'm at her house —"

"Reality check, Alexandra Nicole *Fooling*. Why do I get the feeling you're playing me?"

"You know that old guy at the funeral —"

"Who, Beeson?"

"No, the white-haired doctor, the one I was talking to at the cemetery. He knew my mom, like back in the days. He brought me out here."

"Freeze! That's enough, Als. You stopped being funny about four minutes ago." All of a sudden, Lucinda sounded miffed. "I didn't see any white-haired guy at the cemetery. It was yesterday, so I think I'd remember. Plus, you can't drive from Montana to Massachusetts in one day. And I hope you're not fixing to tell me that he gave you a lift in his private spaceship."

"That's the probs, Luce. I don't know exactly what happened. He packed my bag, and the next thing I remember, I'm ringing Camryn Barnes's doorbell."

"Well, I'm glad you called to tell me all this, especially at five in the morning. Go to bed, Alex. Get some sleep and call me later," Lucinda said and hung up.

Alex was fighting back tears when Cam came out of the bathroom drying her hair. "Bad news?" she asked.

"Only if you call having your best bud think you've gone mental," Alex murmured.

"Don't worry," Cam tried to console her. "I'm sure she'll understand . . . that is, once we figure it out. And there are plenty of kids around here you'll totally like."

"Like Brianna, babe of the bulletins? Hello, I don't think so."

"She's cool — mostly," Cam insisted. "Wait till you meet her and the rest of the crew. There are a bunch of us who hang together. It sounds lame — my dad made this up and it kinda stuck. They call us the Six Pack —"

Alex stuck her finger in her mouth and pretended to gag.

"Well, you're going to have to meet them sometime. I mean, if you're going to be here, be part of —"

Alex interrupted. "I'm not. No offense to the princess pack, but I have plenty of friends back home. And, just so we're clear, I'm not up for adoption."

"I never said you were." Cam was annoyed.

"You never said it, but I know what you're thinking."

"Oh, I forgot, you're the mind reader —"

"Definitely," Alex asserted. "And, in case your — what did your pal Banana call it? Oh, yeah. Your mojo," she mocked. "Well, in case your mojo's on the fritz, you're about to have a visitor!"

"You mean Beth," Cam snapped, wrapping the towel like a turban around her damp head. "As if I didn't know!"

There was a knock at the door. "Cami, you decent? It's me," Beth called.

Cam and Alex both jumped, amazed at the accuracy of their prediction.

"How'd you know?" Cam whispered.

"How did you?" Alex replied.

"I don't know," they both said, scrambling to opposite sides of the room.

CHAPTER TWENTY-TWO
THE SKULL CHARM

Beth saw Alex first, and shrieked. "I can't believe it. You turned yourself into Big Sky-girl. When'd you chop and dye your 'do?"

"Actually, I *am* Big Sky-girl," Alex announced. Her gray eyes sparkling with mischief, she jerked a thumb at Cam. "The leader of the Six Pack is over yonder."

Beth followed the thumb — all the way to Cam, who, looking slightly dazed, flopped down onto her computer chair, still shaken by the accuracy of her guess.

No, it was more than a guess. It had been a certainty. She'd known, just plain known, that the visitor Alex sensed behind the door was Beth — who was now gaping at her, waiting for an explanation.

Cam shrugged sheepishly. "Meet my evil twin?"

Beth wasn't amused. "Drop the flippant." She turned to stare as Alex unzipped the small duffel Doc had packed for her. "Your mom said you had company. But, hello, will someone please tell me what's going on here?"

"Maybe you should sit down," Cam suggested.

Obediently, Beth plopped herself down on Cam's bed.

"It's kind of hard to explain," Cam began. "You remember Alex, right?"

"Well, her face is familiar," Beth cracked dryly. "Hey, hi. Sure I do," she added.

"Bet you didn't expect to see me here." Alex held up a wrinkled blue T-shirt and a pair of weathered cutoffs made from jeans she'd worn till the knees gave out.

"Wow," Beth answered sarcastically. "You totally read my mind."

"Yeah, she's good at that," Cam said. Then, without thinking, she crinkled her nose at the outfit Alex was considering. Which sealed Alex's choice.

"Don't you love these shorts?" Alex crowed to Beth. "Aren't they so, I don't know, so totally un-Marble Bay?"

From the moment she'd entered the room, Beth's mouth had been set in a grimace. Now, as she glanced from Cam to Alex and back again, as she listened to the easy way her best friend and a girl she'd met a week ago bantered with each other, her expression hardened.

"So you guys have kept in touch?" she asked, feeling awkward suddenly, like an outsider, despite the fact that this room was practically her home away from home.

"Not exactly," Alex said.

It didn't help that the real outsider, her best friend's cocky clone, answered the question Beth had totally meant for Cam.

"Well, we did e-mail each other," Cam chimed in.

"Was that before or after you stopped saying how you don't look anything like her?" Beth asked coolly.

"I was wrong. You were right," Cam assured her, feeling the frost in Beth's 'tude. "Honest, Bethie, you have no idea how right."

Instead of melting at the sound of her nickname, instead of gloating or squealing I-told-you-so, Beth stared blankly at her friend.

"Come on, Beth, I thought you'd be psyched." Cam deliberately pumped cheerfulness into her voice. "Don't you get it? Alex and I may really be twins." It didn't work. Why had she thought it would? This was Beth. Not some random person. "It's like you said, back in Montana. You were right. I was adopted. And I never knew it." Cam hadn't expected her voice to crack just then.

But instead of Beth going all buttery, her wiry bud just said, "When did you find out?"

Cam let out a long sigh. "Last night."

"And between last night and this morning, you couldn't find time to tell me?"

Alex rolled her eyes. "She's thrilled, right?"

"Beth, don't be mad —" Cam began.

"I'm not mad," Beth objected. "I'm just, you know, confused."

"Confused?" Alex teased. "Gee, about what?"

"Oh, I don't know," Beth retorted. "How 'bout why my best friend chose not to inform me about two explosions that just rocked her world? You don't think twice about waking me up at four A.M. if you're nervous about a history test! Now you find out, oh, you were adopted! And, in related news, your identical twin, who you refused to admit even looked like you, has popped in for a visit."

Nailed, Cam reached for an excuse. "It all happened so quickly."

"She was here in this room when I called to tell you about the body, wasn't she?"

Cam nodded sheepishly.

Beth's nostrils flared. "And even then, you couldn't tell me?"

"I knew she'd get mad," Alex said. "Lucinda kind of flipped out, too."

"I'm not flipped out." Beth stood up, ticked now that they were talking about her as if she weren't even in the room. "I just don't understand what's going on —"

"Take a number," Alex murmured.

"You know, it's like tuning into a soap opera after missing a bunch of episodes."

"Don't wig," Cam begged.

"Yeah," Alex teased. Tossing her funky Montana duds over her shoulder, she grabbed the cosmetic bag Doc had packed, and sashayed toward Cam's picture-perfect bathroom. "Trust me, Beth. On this soap, we've all missed some crucial episodes."

Alex closed the bathroom door, sat down quickly on the edge of the tub, and pressed the wrinkled blue T-shirt to her face. She inhaled deeply. Under the bitter grease smell of the diner, she breathed in Sara's scent — a vulnerable and tender fragrance of violets, her mother's favorite flower.

Opening the cosmetic bag to find her toothbrush, Alex noticed that Doc had thoughtfully tossed in some of her jewelry. It was a strange selection.

The faded pink silk box that held her mom's delicate moon charm necklace was there. She decided to wear it.

Then she noticed — among worthless hoop earrings, fake rhinestone studs, and the plastic mood ring she'd sported at seven — a miniature silver skull. The one Evan had given her three years ago, when they'd all thought tattoos and body piercing were so in. It was on a tarnished metal chain, as faux silver as the grinning little skull. Alex had nearly forgotten she had it.

The memory of that doofy time, when they'd been such wusses and tried to look so tough, tickled her now. She rubbed the cool little head against her cheek, the way she'd once rubbed the satin trim of her favorite baby blanket. And she thought of chocolaty Evan with his wild dreads and gentle heart.

The ghoulish little trinket was just the thing to go with her rank cutoffs and her mom's sweet-scented old T-shirt. Slipping the necklace over her head, Alex just wished Doc had put in her scuzzy high-tops. They'd have completed the in-your-face look she was after today.

She rummaged through the duffel hoping to find them. No luck, but at the bottom of the bag, she felt a small cool object, which when she pulled it out, turned out to be Doc's quartz crystal.

How he'd sneaked it into her stuff was nearly as mysterious as how he'd got them here in a single day. Alex shrugged, and slipped the beautiful pink stone into the pocket of her shabby shorts.

CHAPTER
TWENTY-THREE
TELL ME WHAT YOU SAW

Beth was just leaving when Alex strutted back into the room, showing off her raggedy Mountain Girl outfit.

"I don't know what you guys are really up to," the lanky girl said, one hand on the doorknob, "but, you know, elsewhere to be!"

"Please, Bethie. Come with us," Cam urged.

"Where, to a medical lab? Sorry I'm going to have to take a Pasadena on that treat. Well, it's been real," Beth said, shaking her head at Alex. "Not unlike that outfit."

"It's the kick, no?" Alex teased, twirling. She felt a stab of sorrow in her gut, the blue-white chill of Beth's distress. The tall, gangly girl was feeling abandoned, Alex realized, left out.

"Seriously," she said quickly. "Come with us. Don't miss out on the lab adventure of a lifetime. Who knows, you might turn out to be my long-lost cousin or something."

Beth hesitated. But, glancing at Cam for encouragement, she caught her best friend shooting her look-alike pal a grateful smile. Beth knew she was being silly, oversensitive, unreasonable. But it hurt, seeing them so comfortable with each other, so close.

"Hang with us. Please, Beth," Cam said.

"Yeah, we'll all get tested," Alex kidded. "They just take a little blood. Dave says all they need is like one cell or something to see if and how we're connected."

"Dave?" Beth stiffened. "Oh, are you and Cam's dad on a first-name basis already? Supposedly you just met him yesterday. I've known him practically all my life. And I still call him Mr. Barnes."

Feeling more excluded than ever, and avoiding Cam's eyes, Beth opened the door. "Well, have fun, you guys," she said too brightly. "Anyway, I really do have to run. I'm baby-sitting."

"Who's the lucky tot?" Cam asked. "One of your regulars?"

Beth paused. Cam was totally making lame conversation, pretending everything was, like, normal. "Jenny McGuire," she finally responded, referring to one of her seven-year-old neighbors.

"Taking her to the duck pond?" Cam probed, adding for Alex's benefit, "We've got this awesome park in the center of town — a huge tire playground, cookout spots, hammocks, and this pond with lots of ducks. Maybe later, we'll stop by, we can show Alex . . ."

"I don't know if I'll take her there. I haven't given it much thought," Beth brushed off the question. "I have to pick her up in a few — so, anyway, bye."

"Is there a chill in the air, or was she just totally bummed to see me?" Alex asked, a moment after the door slammed behind Beth.

"She's not usually like that," Cam said, distressed. "I think she's just —"

"Jealous?" Alex asked. "Wow, I'm getting good. I didn't even have to read your mind for that one."

While Dave filled out dozens of forms for the DNA test, Emily sat uncomfortably in the waiting area of Biogentech labs with the girls, her beloved daughter and the gray-eyed stranger who looked so much like Cam, but was not.

The unknown girl, Alexandra Fielding, was wearing scissored jean shorts and a T-shirt that looked like it hadn't been washed in ages. The girl herself had been sniffing at the shirt whenever she thought no one was watching.

Emily disapproved. Of the child's careless clothing, her offensively dyed hair, her angry independence. And, most of all, of how her presence, her very existence, had unlocked a painful family secret and destroyed the peace and stability of their home.

Yet there was something about the girl that Emily wanted to embrace and protect.

"Are you okay?" she asked, touching Alex's choppy hair, which felt surprisingly soft, like the warm pelt of a wild creature.

Alex pulled her head away. "Sure," she said. Emily's gentle touch unnerved her, felt too weirdly like Sara's caresses.

"We're fine, Mom," Cam said snappishly. It was the first time her daughter had called her Mom since discovering that she was adopted. "Shush," Cam said, eyes fastened on the TV across the waiting room, which was tuned to CNN. "I want to hear this."

As they seemed to be doing every fifteen minutes, the news channel was rehashing the few facts and endless opinions about the dreadful disappearance of Marleigh Cooper, a girl just three years older than Cam.

Alex was squirming, trying to fight back the rising tide of anxiety building in her stomach. She tried to focus on the magazines in the waiting room, on the other patients, anything besides the real reason they were here. Finally, her eye fell on the same TV screen Cam seemed to be glued to.

"Vanished," the announcer was recapping. "The singer left her seat at the soccer game to get better reception on her cell phone. And she hasn't been seen or heard from since. Every day, the mystery deepens."

The actual lab work took practically no time. It was waiting for the doctor to test them that ate up half the day.

It was midafternoon by the time the girls were tested. As promised, there was nothing painful about the procedure. A lab technician took blood samples from each of them. She said she'd be running three different tests and would notify the family when the results were in. "Although," she added, looking from Alex to Cam, "I'd say chances that you two are closely related are pretty good."

"We're going to wait to talk with the doctor," Emily told them, when they walked back out into the marble-floored, icily air-conditioned reception area. "Why don't you girls go out? It's such a gorgeous day. We'll be here for a while."

And find out before us? Cam brooded. And lie to me again, like you did all my life?

"Don't worry." Dave smiled at them. "We'll tell you the absolute truth, just as soon as we know. Which won't be for at least ten days —"

"Promise?" Cam asked.

"Absolutely," Dave said.

When they were outside, standing on the sun-drenched steps of Biogentech, Alex said, "Nice going, dude. Looks like your ESP is kicking into high gear."

"What makes you say that?" Cam asked.

"Your dad didn't say that out loud, that stuff about telling you the absolute truth —"

"But he must have," Cam argued. "I heard him."

"Exactly!" Alex grinned. "You're getting good at it."

"Really?" Cam didn't know whether to be excited or alarmed. She settled for confused.

"Okay, where are we? And what is there to do in this town?" Alex looked up and down the street. A row of shady elm trees dappled the quiet avenue. Flower baskets hung from the whitewashed porches of charming old houses. A salty sea breeze ruffled Alex's hair and delivered to her senses the spicy-sweet tang of well-tended gardens. "You could have your own theme park here," she teased. "Only instead of Big Sky, you'd have to call it Too-

Cute World. What kind of trouble can we get into in a place this quaint?"

"Actually, I know just the thing —"

"The last time someone said that to me," Alex reminded her, "I wound up on your doorstep."

"No, remember that duck pond I was telling you about? We could walk over," Cam ventured.

"And hook up with Beth, right? You're pretty sure that's where she's baby-sitting," Alex said, adding, "you're all bummed about her."

"Look, it's weird for her," Cam started to explain, "but if you don't want to . . ."

"Weird for *her*, huh?" Alex shook her head. "In the lottery of weirdness, she hasn't picked a single number."

" 'Cause you've already got the winning ticket, huh?" Cam knew what Alex was thinking.

"More like the losing one."

Cam felt a stab of guilt. "I didn't mean —"

"Anything by it. I know. Forget it. Suddenly, I have this uncontrollable urge to visit a duck pond."

CHAPTER TWENTY-FOUR
DUCK, DUCK, GOOSE

"Who knows if she'll even be here," Cam murmured as the look-alike teens entered the pond area of the park. Which was, Alex thought, exactly what she imagined it would be. Green, clean, a picture-postcard scene. Just like all of Marble Bay — or what she'd seen so far.

So far . . . as in, far away. From everyone who mattered.

Cam put her hand to her forehead to block the sun from her eyes and scanned the area. Clusters of kids were kneeling by the pond, using remote controls to guide toy boats in the water. Joggers, dog-walkers, kids on scooters, and Rollerbladers shared the path that circled the pond.

Doesn't anyone have to work around here? Alex

wondered, surveying the panorama. On a bench across the pond, she spotted a woman who looked uncannily like her mom. Alex's heart leaped for a second — then turned to stone as she remembered that Sara was gone. Anyway, she reminded herself, even if they'd had a place like this in Crow Creek, Sara wouldn't have been there, reading a book, relaxing on a bench. Two jobs didn't leave time for lightweight luxuries.

The more she saw of Marble Bay, the less she liked it, Alex had decided, when a quick-thudding sound, like a steady drumbeat, interrupted her thoughts. She turned toward the noise, and saw Cam waving and hurrying toward Beth, who she'd just spotted.

She was at a picnic table, talking to a carrottopped kid whose arms and legs were bird-thin. The thudding noise was coming from the child. The little girl's head was down. She was chomping on her fingernails, her legs swinging to the speed-pulsing drum sound.

It was the child who'd attracted her. It was the child's heart she was hearing. The girl was frightened. But her head was down and whatever she was thinking was turning inward, not out. Alex couldn't make out the words.

"Beth!" Cam called out as, trailed by Alex, she came within shouting distance of the pair. "Hey, I hope you don't mind us crashing. Kinda figured you'd be here."

Beth could never mask her feelings. In spite of what had just gone down between them — Cam's bff was clearly stoked to see her. Even if she had brought Alex along.

Beth waved back. "So, how'd the DNA thing go?"

"We won't know anything for a while," Cam answered. "A couple of weeks, I think." Her cell phone rang. "It's Bree," she mouthed after answering it. She motioned for Beth and Alex to come over and listen with her.

Whatever Brianna Waxman had to say held less than zero interest for Alex. The nervous, carrot-topped tot, however, was another story. As Beth listened in on Cam's call, Alex eased herself onto the picnic table bench next to the child.

The little girl was staring down at her hands, fingernails ragged and red. Although she must have known Alex was there, she didn't look up.

"Hey, I'm Alex Fielding. And you're Jenny, right?"

The child didn't respond. But the beating of her fluttering heart grew louder, more panicked.

"You're really sad, aren't you?" Alex pressed gently.

Jenny shrugged. "I was a bad girl," she said.

"Impossible," Alex contradicted the child. "The minute I saw you I knew you were nice. I heard your heart beating fast, and I said to myself, why is that good girl feeling so . . ."

"Bad," Jenny said.

"Well, sad is what I was thinking," Alex said.

"That rhymes," Jenny noted, glancing up at last. "Sad and bad . . ."

And also mad, Alex heard the girl thinking. *I did a very bad thing and now I'm sad. And Marleigh is gone. And everyone's gonna be mad at me.*

"No, they aren't. I'm not," Alex assured the girl.

Jenny looked up suddenly. "Hey, you heard me," she said. Then she saw Evan's necklace, the tarnished little skull hanging from the chain around Alex's neck.

Alex felt Jenny stiffen beside her. Felt a wave of cold fear shudder through the child.

"Jenny, what is it? What's wrong?" she asked.

"You're not nice," the little girl said suddenly, squirming away from Alex. "You're bad. You're bad, too."

"Wow, they're on to him. I can't believe it!" Beth rushed back to the picnic table. "Alex, listen to what Bree just found out."

"It's a Marleigh bulletin, right?" she guessed.

"When Marleigh and I were talking at the game." Cam came over and filled in the blanks. "She said something about a 'fan' of hers who'd been sending spooky e-mail —"

"And the FBI found him!" Beth was pumped. "Well, I mean, they traced the source of the e-mails. They all came from the same computer. Which just so happens to be located right here. In Marble Bay!"

"At the Music & More store," Cam explained.

"Marleigh's mother told the police about the stalker letters she'd been getting," Beth explained.

"And rumor has it, according to Bree, that they were sent from a computer at the Main Street M & M," Cam finished.

"How heinous is that?" Beth demanded, mindlessly stroking Jenny's hair.

Cam's stomach knotted. What did this mean? That her hunch had been dead-on? That Marleigh really *had* been snatched by some sicko who idolized her? The memory of the singer's pale face, when she'd told Cam about the fan who signed his name "Devoted," came flooding back.

Could Cam have prevented anything bad from happening if she'd stayed in town? If she'd listened to the wrinkled old man when he'd said, "*Don't go. She needs you now.*" Those were his words.

But if she hadn't gone on vacation she wouldn't have met Alex.

She needs you now. Those were the same words I

heard, Alex was thinking, that's what the man in my dream told me. But that was before I even knew about Marleigh's disappearance.

Startled, Cam's eyes widened. She zoned in on Alex, who smiled at her. "Did you just say — ?" Cam started to ask.

"Didn't say. Thought," Alex answered aloud.

"Shush," Cam whispered. Okay, this whole mind-reading thing was weirding her out. Even if there was something extremely cool about it.

"The cyber-psycho probably kidnapped her. She's in trouble," Alex said.

"Or was," Beth added, holding Jenny close to her, as if to shield the already frightened child.

"Overreacting much?" Cam struggled to keep the rising panic out of her voice. "Listen to us. If jumping to conclusions was an Olympic event, we'd be Team Gold. We have no idea if any of this is true."

"Don't we?" It was Alex.

CHAPTER TWENTY-FIVE
VOICES IN THE NIGHT

Half Moon Cove was a small crescent of pebbly beach, separated from Marble Bay's main road by a three-foot-high stone seawall. On balmy summer nights, when families with small kids had long gone home, it was a perfect private place for Cam's friends to meet.

Later that night, Cam and Alex decided to hook up with Beth there.

But Beth was nowhere in sight when Dave dropped the girls off.

Decked out in yet another nasty thrift-store ensemble that she'd dug out of her duffel, Alex followed Cam down the mossy stone steps to the cove.

"I'll pick you up around nine-thirty," Dave called after them. "Call if you need a ride sooner."

"I will," Cam answered over her shoulder, before amending, "I mean, we will."

She shot Alex an apologetic look, but the Montana-girl's gaze had already traveled past the beach and was fixed on the bay beyond. A dense mist hung in the early evening air. You could almost stick your tongue out and lick it.

Which Alex seemed about to do.

"Your first beach?" Cam guessed.

"Technically." Alex pressed her lips together and continued to stare straight ahead.

"You never even went to a beach on vacation?" The second it came out of her mouth, Cam wished she could take it back. Way to be insensitive, she berated herself. Alex worked all summer, *and* after school and weekends the rest of the year. There wasn't much time for vacations.

Cam braced herself for a sarcastic comeback, but Alex, walking in step with her toward the shoreline, just said, "We have lakes and streams and all. And this creek not far from home. And —"

"Your mom used to take you there," Cam said.

Alex nodded, then clutched her belly, as if her hands could stop the hollow churning in the pit of her stomach.

"I know that feeling," Cam said, surprising herself as much as Alex. "I've had it, too. That empty feeling. It's homesickness."

"Homesickness?" Alex was nauseated, overwhelmed by the briny smell of the bay. "Trust me, it's not my home I miss — that rancid sardine can in the woods."

Cam touched her elbow. "We don't have to stay here. We can go back, if you want to. I'll square it with Beth. I know this must feel weird —"

"*This* you think is weird?" Less than a month ago, she'd been in Montana, finishing ninth grade, living with her mom, being hassled by a scummy landlord, hanging with her friends. "On the bizarre-o-meter, Barnes, tonight doesn't even register."

For some reason, that struck Cam as funny. "I'm sorry." She clapped her hand over her mouth and apologized for the giggle that escaped her.

"You want to know what's weird?" Alex shot her a lopsided grin. "Your idea of what's weird. Now that's seriously special."

Giddy and tightly wound, Cam tried not to laugh.

With a hard look she couldn't hold, Alex repeated, "Seriously special," then cackled unexpectedly.

Which totally broke Cam up.

"Over here, you guys!" Beth waved to them, setting off a new round of laughter. Clad in denim overalls and a cropped short-sleeved T-shirt, Cam's closest had just gotten there and staked out a spot at the far end of the cove.

They were still laughing when they reached her.

"What's so funny?" Beth sounded cautious.

"Nothing," Cam responded without thinking.

"Nothing *I'd* understand, you mean." Beth tried to make it sound like a joke, but Cam knew her too well.

Reflexively, she took a step away from Alex. "Duh — no. I didn't mean it that way."

"Forget it," Beth said breezily and turned to Alex. "Was this, like, your first dinner at chez Barnes? Did Mrs. B. make her famous chicken parmesan? Oh, wait, I bet Mr. . . . I mean, *Dave*, barbecued. That's what they usually do when Cam has friends over."

"Actually, we had takeout," Cam began, before Beth interrupted.

"Not that you're a friend, exactly. I mean, you're family, right? A sister. A twin. Probably."

Silence, thick as the mist, hung in the air.

Beth cut through it. "Soooo . . . anyway, I heard a little more about the e-mails they traced back to Music & More. The FBI's supposed to be closing in on a suspect."

"The one who called himself 'Devoted'?" Cam asked. "They know who he is? Do they think he kidnapped Marleigh?"

"How can it be a kidnapping? There's no ransom note," Alex pointed out.

"Maybe it's not about money. Maybe he did it for" — Beth clutched her heart dramatically — "love."

Cam and Alex exchanged a glance. Beth was totally trying too hard. It was beyond time for a topic change.

"Speaking of which," Cam said, "Beth thinks this guy Justin in the pizza place likes me."

Beth rolled her eyes. "Okay, first of all, it's Jason. And second of all, yeah, he does. It's so totally obvious."

"To who?" Cam asked. "I mean, what exactly did he say to you?"

To Alex, Beth said, "He's a senior, seventeen, he's got his license, and he's my friend. Of course he tells me stuff."

"About liking me?"

Beth cocked her head. "Not in so many words. But he's given enough hints."

"Hints like he knows what kind of pizza we always order?" Cam asked skeptically.

Beth drew Alex into the convo. "Are you the same as her? I mean, being clueless when some guy really likes you?"

Without meaning to, Alex conjured up a face. Evan's.

And Cam saw it. "He's cute," she said aloud. "I'm not a huge fan of dreads, though, gotta say."

Alex's jaw dropped. "How did you — ?"

"Who are you talking about?" Beth asked, perplexed, looking from one of them to the other. Then a lightbulb went on. "Oh, you mean that guy who was on the Ferris wheel with Alex?"

"Evan," Cam said, relieved. "We met him in the park. Both of us, right, Beth? At Big Sky."

"He's not my boyfriend," Alex protested. "Just a friend. A really, really good friend."

"Who you miss a whole lot, I bet." This time it was Beth who finished the thought.

But it was Cam who understood that dish about Evan was off-limits. Private for Alex. Her world, her friends, her home: She wasn't ready to share them, to open her heart fully to anyone right now. So Cam took the heat off her, switching the subject again. "So the PITS waiter's a senior? Like Tonya. Think he knows her?"

"I doubt it," Beth said. "Tonya the loner doesn't know anyone, really. I mean, she's on our soccer team, but do *we* actually know her? Nuh-*uh.*"

Alex picked up a twig and plopped herself down on the damp beach. Grateful to Cam for changing the topic, she cleared away a patch of pebbles and began making little drawings in the sand. Evan's face. And Luce's. And her mom's.

She tuned in and out of Cam and Beth's discussion. They'd returned to the kidnapping scenario.

So what if Cam "knew" Marleigh had been snatched, Alex brooded. Knowing hadn't stopped it from happening. Knowing didn't get anyone closer to finding Marleigh. Just like Alex's own gifts, her powers, that healing-art thing Doc had talked about — it hadn't helped her save Sara. So what good was any of it?

Please make this all go away. I'm sorry.

Alex looked up to see who'd spoken. The voice hadn't sounded like Cam or Beth.

She strained to hear — what? Something else, someone else . . . But now the message was garbled, staticky, like a radio station caught between signals. Had Cam heard it, too, she wondered, scanning the shadowy beach.

This was so not supposed to happen.

Facing away from Beth and Cam, she heard it more clearly — a fear-choked voice, a girl's. She squinted into the darkness, but the comma of pebbly sand was empty save for the three of them.

Oh, please. I need help. What am I gonna do?

This time, Alex cleared her throat, trying to get Cam's attention. But Cam was hyper-involved with Beth.

If she'd heard the desperate voice, she'd clearly chosen not to react to it.

For Alex, that was not an option. As it always had, the cry of someone in need, a heartfelt plea for help, drew her absolutely. She bounded to her feet, announcing, "I'm gonna take a walk."

Cam looked at her at last. "You want company?"

"No," Alex assured her. "I'm just gonna stretch. Be back soon."

Walking at the water's edge, she concentrated, listening attentively. But now all she heard was the sound of crunching sand pebbles under her feet and the gentle lapping of the bay. She'd walked practically to the opposite end of the beach before she heard it again.

I don't know what to do.

It was coming from the other side of the seawall. Alex dashed toward it.

Please, someone, help me.

She hoisted herself up and over the rocky parapet. Here, there was no beach. Just a wide dirt field, dotted with patches of weeds. No reason for someone to be on this side of the cove, especially at night — unless that someone didn't want to be spotted.

The girl was sitting with her back pressed against the seawall, her head bowed, tangled hair falling over her arms as she hugged her knees. She sobbed softly, barely audibly.

Alex could almost taste her agitated grief, could smell it — piercing and bitter like burnt almonds. "Can I help?" she asked very quietly, hoping not to startle her.

"Huh?" The girl's head jerked up. Panic flooded her round face. "Who's there?"

"I . . . couldn't help hearing —" Alex began.

"Cam? Camryn?" Through her tears, the girl looked up. Squinting, sniffling, she stared at Alex, then unexpectedly giggled. "What happened to you? Did your hair have some unfortunate encounter with a can of blue spray paint?"

Alex sighed, and ran her fingers through her streaked locks. She sat down next to the girl and looked into her eyes, red-rimmed and puffy. And though they'd never met, though the only light available came from moonbeams shafting through the clouds, she got it.

So this was Tonya Gladstone.

CHAPTER TWENTY-SIX
TESTING TONYA

"It's . . . Tonya, right?"

"Duh," Tonya sniffed, using the sleeve of her pullover to wipe her eyes, "Did someone dare you to do that to your hair? And why are you wearing that hanging skull thing, and that . . . uh . . . getup? Where'd you get them — at the Salvation Army?"

Alex took a deep breath. Funny. She didn't feel dissed at all — she felt too sorry for the girl.

Before she could find out why Tonya had been crying inconsolably, she'd have to explain herself. "I'm actually not Cam," she started.

Tonya blew her nose. "And I'm actually not Alice. And this is not actually Wonderland."

"Look, I know you're gonna find this really, really hard to believe. . . ."

In the end, words weren't enough. Alex had to practically drag Tonya over the seawall, back to Cam and Beth. Tonya kept looking from Cam to Alex in shock and disbelief.

Which was why it struck Alex as odd that the distraught girl's astonishment dissolved completely the minute Beth let her in on the music store computer news. *That* sent shock waves through Tonya.

"I don't believe it!" she exclaimed. "They can't trace where an e-mail came from. That's impossible! No way!"

"Wa-a-ay," Beth needled her. "It takes a while, but these e-detectives or whatever they call them, can track down that server thingie, and from there, find the actual computer the e-mail was sent from."

"Lucky for Marleigh," Cam said.

"Lucky? Only if it's not too late," Beth reminded them.

Tonya shivered and drew her sleeve up to blot her face. "It's all my fault. I feel so responsible," she whimpered. "If it wasn't for me, Marleigh wouldn't have come here. Now it's like I led her to her . . . I don't know what!"

Cam touched Tonya's hand. "It's not your fault. You couldn't have known what would happen."

"Unless, of course," Beth probed, "you told someone at Music & . . ."

"Did not!" Tonya's tone was suddenly defensive.

"Down, girl. No one said you did. She was just wondering," Alex said.

Tonya turned contrite. "Sorry. It's just that it was supposed to be a surprise. I wanted to do something cool for the team, for our championship game. And Marleigh was such a good sport! She wanted to be this good-luck charm, as a favor to me. And now this happened."

As a favor to Tonya, Cam thought. But why? There were lots of regional fan club presidents; surely Marleigh didn't hop on a plane every time one beckoned. Again, Cam remembered the "it's so tragic" remark Marleigh had made about Tonya. Was there some kind of connection?

Beth suddenly thought of something. "Hey, Tonya, isn't there some guy you're friends with at Music & More? That guy with the . . ." She suddenly flipped around, pointed at Alex's necklace, and made a face. "Dangling earring. A nasty skull — like that."

A memory of the scared little girl from the playground flashed across Alex's inner radar. Unconsciously, she covered the necklace with her hand.

Tonya's eyes hardened. "If you're talking about the clerk at Music & More, I think his name tag says Kevin. Which is all I know about him."

"Think he sent the e-mails?" Beth asked.

"Puh-leeze. That nitwit couldn't figure out how to turn on a computer, let alone compose an e-mail," Tonya snapped. "He's a lowlife. How could he appreciate someone like Marleigh?"

"Hey, it's okay if you accidentally let it slip that she was coming to town," Cam tried to reassure the agitated girl. "No one's holding you responsible."

"I didn't let it slip!" Tonya exploded. "I told you — I never said a word to anyone. I just tried to do something good. And now you're all acting like I'm a criminal or something. . . ." She broke down sobbing. Instantly, Cam rushed to her side, Alex took her hand.

"Hey," Cam asked when Tonya ran out of tears, "how 'bout if we take you home? I'll call my dad for a ride now."

Back in Cam's room later, Alex kicked off her sandals and stretched out on the spare bed. It was hers, she guessed, temporarily, anyway. She turned her head toward the window; the glow of the moon seemed to pull at her. It was hard to believe it was the same moon that shone over Crow Creek, which seemed worlds away. Where everyone was so different from the people she'd met here. . . . Take Tonya, for instance. The unhappy girl was obviously rich. They'd dropped her off in front of a sprawling mansion that sat up on a hill, behind huge iron gates.

"I guess sad-sack Gladstone is really loaded, huh?" Alex mused idly.

Cam was sitting in her swivel chair, booting up her laptop. Checking her e-mail before she went to bed was a nightly ritual. Her back to Alex, she shrugged. "I guess." The cacophonous blare of the modem connecting — which always reminded Cam of a flock of bleating geese — filled the room.

"But her crib," Alex practically had to shout over the noise, "I've seen hotels smaller."

Cam clicked onto her e-mail account. There were, like, three from Dylan. Unsurprisingly, her kid brother had been blindsided by the double dose of news — about her being adopted, and about Alex. He wanted to come home, but their parents had insisted he stick it out the one more week of camp. Now, he was full of Alex questions.

Cam hit REPLY, and started to answer. To Alex, she absently said, "Tonya's family probably has more than your average millionaire. But it's not like money buys happiness. Obviously."

"Yeah, obviously. Maybe all it buys you is better medical care."

Cam's fingers froze on the keyboard. She swiveled around in her chair. "My bad. I so didn't mean anything."

"I know you didn't," Alex admitted, propping herself up on her elbows. "It's cool, forget it."

Cam drew her knees up on the chair. "You know, not everyone around here is as weird as Tonya. There are actually some kids you'd probably really get along with —"

"Members of the Slick Pack, I presume. Don't sweat it. Besides" — Alex turned away from Cam — "it's not like I'm staying. No matter what the DNA results show."

Surprised at how bruised she felt, Cam turned back to her PC. A moment later, she swiveled around to face Alex. "You didn't just stumble on Tonya when you took that walk, right? Even though that's what you made it seem like."

"I heard Tonya crying . . . I guess you didn't?"

"No," Cam admitted through gritted teeth. "Excuse me, I guess I'm just not as sensitive as you."

"Don't stress," Alex counseled, reading her mind. "If you weren't so deep into it with Beth, so big-time involved, babbling about boys, you would've heard her, too. Probably."

Cam said defensively, "I asked if you wanted company." She jumped off her chair and walked over to the window.

"Hey, it's no big." Alex swung her legs over the side of the bed. "Beth is your best friend. And this" — she swept her arm around the room — "is your life. Even if," Alex anticipated Cam's comeback, "you always thought you were Dave and Emily's biological child. Now you find out . . . uh, not so fast. You know what? Nothing's really gonna change for you. You'll forgive them, you'll go back to your regularly scheduled world, starring soccer mom, good-lawyer dad, tousle-headed little brother. Me, I'm just passing through."

"Great!" Cam hollered, stung. "Maybe before you cut out, you could tell me what Tonya was saying. What exactly did you hear that made you want to go find her?"

Alex was taken aback. She hadn't meant to hurt Cam, could hardly believe that she even could. And now Little Miss Sunshine was snapping on her. Alex sighed, "Tonya was going, 'I'm sorry, I never meant for this to happen.' She was incredibly sad."

"With good reason. Marleigh. She's . . ." Cam paused. "I know you're gonna say, another 'poor little rich girl.' But it's not like that. At least, it didn't seem that way when I talked to her. She was really sweet."

Alex didn't respond right away.

But Cam knew what she was thinking. "I know you don't care all that much about the whole Marleigh thing. But right now? It *is* kinda easier than talking about . . . you know . . . us."

"Bull's-eye," Alex agreed. She sighed, "I know you told the police everything you remember about the fateful day, but rewind the tape. Who knows, maybe . . ." She trailed off.

Cam picked up the thread. "Between the two of us, we can figure something out? You're kidding, right?"

Alex shrugged. "Humor me. Tell me exactly what you saw."

So Cam reviewed the day of the soccer disaster, about how Tonya had sprung this incredible surprise by bringing Marleigh Cooper to the game. About how Tonya then pretended she and Cam were friends, and insisted on a photo op. And then about doing face-time with Marleigh, and how the singer, in fact, seemed like a genuinely nice person.

Sarcastically, Alex said, "So did you and your glitzy new best friend exchange cell phone numbers? Make plans to double-date with 'N Sync?"

Cam folded her arms. "Very funny. Right after the photo was taken, Marleigh went back into the stands with Tonya."

Alex finished, "The very stands from which she'd soon vanish."

Cam nodded and continued, "As Tonya told the police, Marleigh needed to make a call and couldn't get reception on her cell phone from her seat, so she went down to the parking lot."

Alex tilted her head and pursed her lips.

"What?" Cam asked.

"Glub, glub . . ."

"Glub?" Cam repeated. "In our language, please."

Alex laughed, "Something sounds fishy. That's what my homeys do when we don't believe something. Anyway, go on. What happened on the field?"

Although it still bummed her to repeat the story, Cam told Alex about how Lindsay had cried foul and accused Cam of blinding her. And about how she'd choked and never made the goal to keep her team alive.

"Why'd you choke?" Alex asked gently.

"Because something made me look up in the stands — right that second."

"Where you saw?" Alex prodded.

"I saw this kid, this child — well, no more than a flash of curly red hair — scampering down the bleachers." Cam stopped abruptly. She hadn't told the police about that — because she'd forgotten it. Somehow, talking to Alex made her remember things she hadn't before.

Alex searched Cam's eyes. "A kid running made you choke? What else did you see up there, Cam?"

A man, the crinkly-faced man from my dreams.

And suddenly there he was in the stands, telling me not to leave. To stay because Marleigh needed me. Well, I thought he meant Marleigh, but he could have meant you — Alex — too.

Cam never actually said those words out loud. She didn't have to. Alex had read her mind.

"This decrepit dude, what kind of hair did he have?"

Taken aback, Cam bristled, "When I want you to read my mind, I'll inform you. Otherwise, cease and desist, okay?"

"Adjust," Alex advised her. "Was his hair, like, pure white but kind of wild, like windblown cotton?"

Cam nodded.

"Was he funny-looking? Skinny, but strong in a way?"

"Well, he wasn't exactly ha-ha funny-looking. And who's Doc?"

Now it was Alex's turn to be had. "I was thinking it was Doc — I didn't say it was."

"And I read your thoughts," Cam bragged, "so like you said, adjust. And tell me who Doc is."

"The weird old guy who brought me here." Alex gulped suddenly.

"Did you ever see him at night?" Cam was almost afraid to ask, "I mean, you know, like in a dream?"

What came flooding back to Alex filled her face with grief. Doc. Why hadn't she put it together before?

Wasn't he one and the same as the pasty-faced old guy with the raspy voice, who'd warned her to stay close to Sara? If she'd listened to him . . .

The pain on her look-alike's face stopped Cam from reading Alex's mind. Whatever was hurting the mother-less child was too much to bear. Instead, Cam whispered, "You know, I thought I was losing my mind when I saw him in the stands."

"You weren't," Alex assured her. Then, because she just couldn't help herself, added, "All you were losing was the game!"

Cam tried to grimace, but broke out laughing in-stead. "Way to add a little levity." And the truth was, for the first time in a long time, Cam felt like a weight had been lifted. Just being able to tell Alex everything — all the things Beth and her parents would not believe — al-lowed Cam to feel free somehow.

Much later, after Cam had shut the lights and spent a restless half hour staring at the ceiling, watching tree shadows sway in the moonlight, Alex whispered, "Are you awake?"

Cam snorted, "Rhetorical-question-alert. You know I am."

"I just thought of something."

"I hope it's a short thought. It's really late and I'm fried."

Alex sat upright in bed. "When you were telling me about Marleigh's vanishing act, you said the white face, the bleacher-creature, forced you to look up in the stands. Tell me again what you saw — I mean, besides him and the little kid who was running."

Cam flipped from her back onto her side and yawned. "Just what I told you. Marleigh was gone. Nightmare man had taken her place next to Tonya —"

"What was Tonya doing?" Alex leaned forward.

"What do you mean? She was watching the game. Watching me blow the game, if that's what you're getting at —" Cam sat up. "Okay, even though Tonya wasn't playing because of her ankle, she was wearing her team uniform. Her crutches were propped up next to her."

"Was she screaming, like, go, team, go? Or some lame cheer?" Alex prompted.

"Yeah, really lame." Cam almost laughed, remembering how Tonya wildly shrieked, "Kill them!" But that was earlier. When Marleigh left . . . "She was on the phone," Cam recalled.

"Her cell phone?"

"Okay, okay, we're all tech trendoids — go on, say it."

But Alex wasn't thinking about that. "You just said Marleigh needed to make an important call and couldn't get reception. Tonya had suggested she try going behind the stands. And no one saw her ever again."

Camryn Barnes and Alexandra Fielding had identical reactions. "How come Tonya's phone worked just fine in the stands —" Alex wondered aloud.

Cam finished the thought. "And Marleigh's didn't?"

CHAPTER TWENTY-SEVEN
AN ENCHANTMENT
FOR JENNY

"We have to tell someone," Cam said, for the fifth time, as she poured cereal into twin bowls.

It was Sunday morning, and the girls had slept in. Dave and Emily had left a note reminding Cam they were at their weekly tennis game and would be back in a few hours.

"Sure we do," Alex, who was perched on a tall stool by the kitchen counter, sarcastically replied. "We should tell, oh, I don't know, your parents? The police? How 'bout the media? And you're going to say exactly what? That you saw — in exquisite, minute detail — what you were totally too far away to have possibly seen? Tonya on her cell phone?"

Cam put the cereal box down and frowned. Alex was right, of course. From her position on the field, no way could anyone see that much detail in the bleachers. No one *normal*, that is. She sighed.

"While you're on the topic," Alex teased, "why not tell everyone about what happened at Big Sky? How we saw and heard what we couldn't possibly have, how we mended the rusted Ferris wheel bolts? You can even throw in the part about the rhyming thing."

Cam gulped. She still had no clue why, at certain times, these rhymes, or as Alex called them, incantations, popped into her head.

Alex flipped on the kitchen TV. She channel surfed, but couldn't get away from what had become a national obsession. Regurgitating the same old, same old. The singer had vanished. She'd been getting strange e-mails. Which they'd traced to a computer in town. And that's where the trail went cold.

Cam grabbed spoons and brought their breakfast to the table. "Snag the milk, okay?" She nodded at the fridge.

Alex opened the refrigerator door. She was nearly blinded by the white, bright, spilling over-fullness of it all. Containers of juice and milk, bottled water, cold cuts wrapped in crinkly waxed paper, a loaf and a half of bread, eight bottles of salad dressing lined up in the shelf on the door, plastic containers of leftovers.

A picture of her own pitiful half-fridge in the trailer came to her. The wilted lettuce, the pocked tomato, the mostly empty jar of peanut butter — clear evidence that something was wrong, that her mom wasn't taking care of business. That she was going downhill fast. Why hadn't Alex picked up on the clues, and insisted that Sara be seen at the clinic immediately?

She didn't mean to slam Cam's fridge shut, but apparently, she did. Hard enough to rattle the salad dressing bottles.

Cam whirled around, annoyed. "It can break, you know."

"So?" Alex, whose heart was breaking just that second said, "Just get a new one. What's it to you?"

Cam closed her eyes. Was this how it was going to be every single day? She almost wished Alex had never shown up. And that she'd leave. Soon.

But Alex copped to her bad right away. "That remark, as my teacher Miss Flock used to say, was totally uncalled for, young lady. I'm sorry, Camryn. Anyway, it was an accident. I didn't mean to slam it. I barely touched it." Opening it slowly now, she was relieved to see nothing had smashed.

"I know you didn't. C'mon, have some cereal. It's my signature dish."

Alex laughed. "No-can-cook, huh? I'll have to teach you."

"What's your specialty?"

"Oh, you know," she said with a mischievous twinkle. "Fried pig, opossum tails, deer brains. Just the usual for us hicks."

"Cute, remind me to get the reci —" Cam stopped mid-quip. The voice coming from the TV screen was too familiar. Tonya, being interviewed outside her house.

"I can't believe those news goons are stalking her," Cam said indignantly. "And hello, Sunday! Can't they give it a rest?"

Alex shook her head. "She knows more than she's saying."

"What are *you* saying? That Tonya had something to do with Marleigh's disappearance? Your mojo's in no-go, Alex."

Alex lifted the cereal bowl to her mouth and gulped down the last of the milk. Something Cam used to do before Dylan started imitating her.

"Right. I'm just a clueless yokel from Montana," Alex said, wiping her mouth with the napkin. "But you said no one knows her all that well, right?"

Cam sighed. "What I said was, she's a loner. It doesn't make her capable of . . . you know."

Alex shrugged, grabbed both their bowls, and went to the sink to wash them.

"You don't have to do that," Cam said, following her. "I'll get 'em."

"I'm not chore-allergic," Alex said sharply. "Or, for that matter, too fragile to earn my keep. Speaking of which, would you know if there are any baby-sitting gigs up for grabs?"

"I guess. Why?"

"I need a job."

"You do?" Cam chuckled. "I thought you weren't staying."

"I'm not. Not forever, anyway. But since I don't know how I got here, obviously, I can't get back the same way. And without money, I'm stuck here."

Cam grabbed a towel and furiously wiped the bowls dry. "My parents will give you money. If you want to leave that bad."

Alex's voice softened. "Look, I have to stay at least until the DNA results come back. And I'm used to working. It's what I do. Anyway, it looked like fun — I'd rather be minding kids than stuck in that suffocating ticket booth at cheesy old Big Sky."

Cam smiled. "You like kids, huh?"

"I really do," Alex conceded. "You know that kid Jenny, the one Beth baby-sits? She's hyper-freaked about the Marleigh thing."

"Everyone in town is — in case you hadn't noticed."

"There's something else going on. Poor kid has this twisted idea it's her fault Marleigh vanished."

Now Cam put down the dishes. "Excuse me, you spent like a half second with this child. And somehow, you know all this already?"

Softly, Alex said, "She's a mess. Beth knows it. She just doesn't know why, let alone how to help her."

It took only a second for Cam to recognize the look in Alex's eyes. "You have a hunch, don't you? You think Jenny, a seven-year-old, knows something about Marleigh."

"All I know is this: Jenny is one terrified little chickadee. Maybe she saw something, maybe not. But if I can help her, I want to. I want us both to."

"What can we do?" Cam challenged. "It's awful that Jenny somehow blames herself for Marleigh's disappearance. But where do we come in? We're not shrinks or anything. We're just kids — with problems of our own."

"You and me," Alex said, staring hard at Cam. "Whoever we are really? We are anything but 'just kids.'"

*   *   *

Thirty minutes later, after getting the address from Beth, they were ringing the bell at Jenny's house. It fell to Cam, who had met the girl's parents once, to get them in the door. And while Cam chatted with Jenny's mom — explaining how they'd noticed Jenny was pretty upset yesterday and thought they could get her to open up about what was bothering her — Alex would talk to Jenny again and try to help her.

Alex found Jenny in her bedroom. The walls were plastered with pictures. Some were the child's own crayoned artwork on construction paper, others were glossies of Marleigh Cooper, cut out of magazines. Jenny was still in bed, wearing pajamas.

She was clutching a book, her hair an uncombed ball of frizz-curls.

"Hey, Jenny." Alex waved from the doorway. "Remember me? We met at the duck pond, yesterday."

Jenny's pale blue eyes took Alex in. Her birdlike body stiffened.

Memories of her own sickening childlike terror, when Hardy Beeson would stand in the door frame, with that twisted look on his face, demanding money, came flooding back to Alex. She didn't want to scare the tousled tot. "Is it okay if I come in?" she asked, smiling. "Your mommy said I could talk to you for a minute. But if you don't want, that's cool. I'll just go."

She held her breath. But Jenny didn't boot her. Instead she whispered into her book, "You could stay."

"Thank you," Alex said, walking over to the bed. "I wanted to ask you something. What made you say I was bad yesterday? I know you didn't really mean it. I'm a friend of Beth's, and you like her, right?"

Jenny glanced up at Alex finally. "Beth's nice. We're friends."

"I'd like to be your friend, too. If that's okay with you."

Jenny shrugged her narrow shoulders and buried her head deeper into her book.

Alex checked its cover. The Powerpuff Girls. Cartoon characters. "You like that story?" she ventured. "Can you read it all by yourself?"

Jenny didn't respond. Alex tried again. "In the picture, it looks like The Powerpuff Girls are flying. Are they superheroes?"

Jenny slammed the book shut, pressed her lips together, and stared out the window.

Way to be lame, Alex reprimanded herself. Like pretend-bonding over a book would magically make this kid open up. Could she get any more *Touched by an Angel*? Alex almost laughed. Like that would've worked with her? Never! Kids always know when you try to manipulate them. Alex dropped the coy.

"Jenny, can you just look at me for a minute?" Gently, she reached out and lifted the child's chin. Jenny didn't resist. But the little girl's eyes never reached Alex's face: They froze when they got to her necklace. Jenny started to shake.

That boy! That bad boy! I don't like him!

Had Jenny said that or only thought it? Alex was pretty sure it was the latter. "Jenny, sweetie," she explained, "this is just a silly charm. I know it looks scary, but it can't hurt you. It's just tin, like a toy."

Jenny swallowed and gripped her book so tightly, the tips of her bitten-off fingernails whitened. Her heart began to beat wildly. *He took her away!*

Alex's stomach twisted. She pushed on, trying to keep her voice light. "Lots of people wear them. It doesn't mean they're bad. Some people wear them as earrings. Even boys! Isn't that silly?"

Jenny's silence filled the room, but Alex didn't want to stop. "Guess what. I'm new in Marble Bay. But I heard there's a boy who works at the CD store. A tall boy who wears an earring just like this. I bet you saw him when you went to buy Marleigh's record, right?"

Suddenly, Jenny shook her head vigorously. At the mention of Marleigh's name, pools of tears formed in her perfectly round blue eyes. "My mommy bought me her song."

Alex took a sharp breath. "You never went into the CD store? It's called Music & More?"

Jenny didn't answer. Alex continued, "But you know the boy I'm talking about, don't you?"

The trembling little girl folded her bony arms across her chest. "I'll get in trouble if I say."

"I promise I won't tell anyone if you don't want me to. But this is for Marleigh. Maybe we can help find her. Where did you see this boy?"

"Go away now!" Jenny suddenly erupted, balling her hand into a fist. "I don't want to talk to you anymore!"

"Hey, Jen." The voice came from the doorway: It was Cam's and she kept it level, casual. "That's okay. You don't have to talk to her if you don't want to."

Alex glared at Cam. *But it would be really important if she did! She saw something the day Marleigh disappeared. I'm sure of it. The kid's in big trouble. I'm doing my best to help her. Think you can do better?*

Alex had thought that, spoken to Cam in silence. And Cam had heard it clearly. She was getting pretty cool at this. Furtively, she glanced around the room. Was there something she could do to win Jenny's trust, to get her to open up?

Her eye fell on one of the crayon drawings on the wall, a rainbow over a girl with long yellow hair. Cam realized the crudely drawn figure was Jenny's rendition of Marleigh.

Enchant her!

Huh? Who'd said that? Not Alex. Her look-alike hadn't even *thought* that.

Yet the voice — how weird! — sounded familiar.

Enchant her? What did that mean? Delight her? Dazzle her? What would enchant a seven-year-old? Cam had an idea. A dumb one, maybe — but it was the only one she could scrounge up on short notice.

She stared hard at the child's drawing of Marleigh. She gazed intently at the rainbow. But nothing happened, nothing changed. Then she felt the heat rising in her again. Easy, she told herself, not too hot . . . Cam's eyes stung and began to tear. The rainbow blurred.

She blinked desperately, trying to focus again. And then it happened, she could see it happening. One by one, the colors of Jenny's rainbow grew vivid, began to shine, shimmer, sparkle! Excellent! Over the yellow-haired Marleigh, a now-glittering rainbow arched.

Cam was about to give herself major kudos, but there was one problem. Her enchanted picture was still on the wall: Jenny didn't see it.

Alex did. And remembered how her thoughts had made a spoon fly once. But would her wish to help a fearful child be as powerful as her rage at Beeson? Could she make something move out of love instead of hate?

"Help me," she whispered to no one in particular, and stared at the twinkling drawing. A gentle breeze wafted through the room. The tape at the corners of the picture curled. The paper lifted away from the wall and sailed gently over to the bed, landing on the child's lap. And for the first time in what Alex guessed was a long time, little Jenny's face lit up.

"Look! My drawing is sparkling! I didn't even put glitter on it! It's magic!"

Alex grinned. "What a cool drawing. Anyone can tell it's Marleigh Cooper."

They'd gotten Jenny to loosen up. Could they get her to open up?

Enchant her. The voice again. And Cam thought of the rhyme, the spell Alex had recited Friday night.

"Oh, sun that gives us light and cheer, shine through me now to banish fear," Cam began to chant.

And then she stopped, spacing out on the rest.

Alex froze. Cam was doing Doc's incantation! Bad plan! She hadn't told Cam that it only worked if you believed in magic. Cam was trying to do it for real. Alex was about to stop her when she looked at Jenny's glowing face. They had made her picture sparkle and had set it in her lap. The *child* believed in magic. Maybe that was enough.

Grasping the quartz crystal in her pocket, Alex finished, "Free young Jenny from doubt and blame; let us win her trust and lift her shame."

Jenny looked up. Her thin voice wavered. "I did a bad thing. Mommy said don't leave the seat . . ."

"Your seat at the soccer game?" Cam moved closer to the bed, and now stood right next to Alex. "You were at the game?"

Jenny burst into tears. "Mommy said, 'Stay here.' But Marleigh was walking away. I just wanted to say hi."

Cam fished a tissue out of her tote and handed it to Alex, who reassured the child, "It's okay, honey. No one's going to tell on you."

"Are you twins?" Jenny, momentarily distracted, asked.

Cam and Alex answered at the same time. "We think so."

Jenny brightened. "Like Mary-Kate and Ashley?"

"Exactly," Cam answered as Alex rolled her eyes. "We're just like them."

"Sweetie, did you leave your seat to follow Marleigh? And is that when you saw the boy with the earring like this? He went somewhere with Marleigh?"

"Mommy went to get me ice cream. I just wanted Marleigh's autograph."

"I saw you," Cam said suddenly. "I mean, that was you. That flash of red curls . . ."

Alex shot her a look so clear Cam didn't need mind-reading skills. *Put a cork in it,* it said. *We're finally getting somewhere.*

"Did you get her autograph?" Alex continued. "Can I see it?"

From under her pillow, Jenny retrieved a napkin, crumpled now, and offered it to Alex. "'To Jenny. I'm so happy to meet you!'" Alex read aloud. "'I love your freckles. Stay smiling. Love, Marleigh.'"

CHAPTER TWENTY-EIGHT
MUSIC & SO MUCH MORE

Their first stop after Jenny's house was Music & More.

They parked their bikes — Alex had borrowed Dylan's — in the rack outside the store. "Okay, I'll do the talking," Alex announced, heading inside.

Cam scurried after her. "Not! As in, not okay. You just got here —"

"Yeah, yeah, I know. While you're the teen queen of Marbled Brains. But in this case, being an outsider might be helpful. Trust me, Cami."

"Trust you? Why? Because you were so successful getting Jenny to open up all by yourself?" Cam allowed herself a tiny smirk.

"Oooo. Vicious," Alex mocked. "Just watch me and learn." Before Cam could respond, she hurried up to the register, where the lone clerk was playing with a palm-sized video game.

Propping her elbows on the counter, Alex batted her eyes at the boy. "I was looking for Kevin," she crooned. "But you're way cuter." He looked up, gasped faintly, dropped the game with a clatter, and clutched the pencil protector in the shirt pocket over his heart.

"Kevin doesn't work here anymore," he reported, his voice cracking. "Can I help you?"

"Hope so," Alex purred.

Behind her, Cam made a gagging sound.

"Wow, is that the computer they traced Marleigh's fan mail to?" Running her fingers lovingly along the edge of the PC on the counter, Alex beamed at the boy.

"Uh, no. The FBI took that one." Blushing, he noticed Cam, making faces behind Alex's back. "Oh, you guys are twins —"

"I never saw her before in my life," Cam snapped, turning away to study a rack of CDs. "This ploy is so doomed," she muttered.

Alex shot the clerk a big smile. "Will you excuse me?" she asked sweetly. Her smile frosted as she glared over her shoulder at Cam. "Put a sock in the mock, Barnes. Five minutes. That's all I need."

Five minutes got her only so far. Got the M & M man to tell them that the computer the FBI had seized used to be in the back room that only employees had access to. And that Kevin Bullock, the ex-clerk who wore the skull earring, had gone AWOL just days before the Marleigh tragedy. Which was probably why the cops suspected him of being the whacked-out fan.

But they were way off base, the pencil protector had assured Alex — because Kevin was borderline illiterate, totally incapable of operating a computer. And, well, yeah, if he'd really wanted to send e-mail, he could have maybe gotten someone to help him . . .

"But, hey," the young clerk said as three kids charged into the store, laughing and punching one another, "I'd better get back to work —"

"Just a few more minutes, please," Alex urged.

"Look, I'm really sorry, but I could get canned if the boss walked in now. I'm not even supposed to talk about this stuff —" The clerk started toward the rowdy boys.

"Wait." Cam spun around suddenly. "She — I mean, we —" she said in a silky soft voice, "just need a teeny bit more of your time."

The clerk turned to glance at her. Cam flashed her eyes at him. "Blunder and stumble," she recited. "Um, let the fun begin."

She had him! She could feel it, feel her eyes begin to

sting. See the boy's surprised stare — a second before he tripped, and like Lindsay at the finals, keeled forward with a bang.

"What did you just do?!" Alex demanded, helping the stunned clerk to his feet.

"Bought us a bonus round," Cam said.

Which was how they learned that, yeah, there was this kid who was always buying Kevin stuff, and who used to hang out at the store. With Kevin — who, by the way, was definitely not your "Devoted" fan of anything Marleigh Cooper — especially not her bubblegum brand of music. The only thing Kevin was devoted to was bragging.

"What'd he have bragging rights to, exactly?" Alex asked.

"Nothing real. Just this dumb little fantasy, about how as soon as he got enough money, he was gonna get himself a motorcycle, move out of his parents' place, and live on his own . . ."

The clerk kept going, but Cam had tuned out. She could hear him speaking but couldn't make out the words. Then her vision went blurry again. And her head started to pound. And she saw a narrow, no-lane, dirt road, winding around a curve. It seemed to be in some untended wooded area, overgrown. Just beyond the curve there was something, a building, a sign, but Cam couldn't make it out. Her vision sharpened. For a split

second, she saw what looked like . . . a rusty, old gas station pump . . . a boarded-up bunker in the woods . . . and
a sign. END — Then the mirage shattered.

End . . . of what?

"So what'd the rich guy look like?" Alex was asking
the dazed clerk. "You know, the one who hung out with
Kevin in the back room —"

"Wasn't a guy. It was a girl," the boy answered.
"Kinda chunky kid. Looked a lot like the one who's supposed to have brought Marleigh to the game. You know
who I mean? That girl who's always crying on TV . . ."

Cam could barely hide her glee as the girls left the
store. "Whoo-*hoo*! I am good! I totally got him. All I had to
do was dazzle the boy. Give him a little Lindsay eye-lock
action. Just stare him down and think really hard."

Alex frowned. "Want to back it up there? Who got
him to open up? In spite of you grunting and gagging
every five seconds."

"Whatever." Cam threw her head back, brushing a
hank of auburn hair out of her eyes. "So maybe you did
the talking — if that's what you want to call it. I mean,
Alex, eew, that was rank."

Alex sniffed. "Watch it, Camryn, your snob is showing. A clerk's not cool enough for you? Doesn't hold a
candle to pizza-boy, right? And what was that crack when

he asked if we were twins? You said you'd never seen me before. *That* was believable."

"It wasn't that much of a stretch." Cam laughed. "I've never seen you act like that before. Anyway, we better go home now."

"Back to your house? Are you nuts? After everything we just found out?"

"Look, maybe you don't care, but my parents are gonna be worried. We didn't even leave a note; they have no idea where we are."

Impatiently, Alex snapped, "So call them. Where's that famous cell phone when you need it? Don't you get it? We're on to something here. We can't just go home now. As you'd put it, 'elsewhere to be.'"

Cam strolled over to the bike rack. "Maybe I used up my mojo in M & M, but right at this moment, I don't know what you're thinking —"

"Come on, use a grain of brain." Alex sighed. "The kid said, yeah, maybe Kevin-the-missing got someone to help him. Okay, he couldn't use the back-room computer. But maybe he let a friend — a friend, who, I don't know, has tons of money and might've slipped him a Benjy or two every once in a while? You know, for his motorcycle-fantasy fund. Maybe he let this customer, this moneyed pal of his, use it." She paused. "You know as well as I do, Camryn, it's time we paid a visit to too-strange Tonya."

CHAPTER TWENTY-NINE
THE COUNCIL

"May the wisdom and the courage of our forebears be with us this day. The Coventry Island Unity Council will now come to order."

The short, stout woman with her cocoa complexion and wiry — some would say unruly — mass of steel-gray hair stood dead center on the floor of the amphitheater. Her ample mulberry robe billowed as she spun around, clapping her dimpled hands, demanding the attention of everyone in the circular arena.

Her name was Rhianna; her title, Exalted Elder. Today, she was presiding over a hastily called emergency meeting of the Coventry Island Unity Council.

It was a meeting Ileana had insisted upon.

And Karsh had reluctantly agreed to.

Once he'd admitted to Ileana that the twins were together, Ileana demanded to be informed of their every move.

"Come see for yourself," Karsh had invited her, but the hot-tempered young witch had waved him off. "Tracking them is your job," she'd insisted. "As is reporting to me."

And so Karsh had.

With unmasked pride, he'd told her how the girls seemed to fit together as seamlessly as their baby necklaces; how Camryn's protector, Dave, had sensed that the one called Alex was as his own daughter and had welcomed her into their home; how Alex was grieving the loss of Sara; and how both girls, in time-honored fashion, were drawn toward helping others and had become involved in trying to solve a mysterious disappearance.

That last bit, Karsh realized too late, was probably what the kids called the EMI or TMI — Too Much Info — for Ileana had arched a perfectly shaped eyebrow and demanded details.

Which was when Karsh had foolishly told her about the gummy princess, or was it the chewing-gum diva — some such phrase — who'd been snatched practically before Camryn's eyes. By herself, the accomplished child had been helpless to prevent it. But now that Alex was with her, the twins were using their combined powers to search out and save the singer.

That's when Ileana exploded. Normally, the self-absorbed witch couldn't be bothered with news of the outside world. But she'd recently come from Los Angeles, where the showbiz snatching had been Topic A outside of the spell-casting seminar.

"They're involved in the Marleigh Cooper debacle?" Ileana had raged. "Every news crew in the world is covering that case. Could you find a more high-profile event for them to be mixed up in? What's your next brilliant plan, Karsh? To send an engraved invitation to Thantos?"

Ileana's thundering rant had concluded with, "I demand you remove Artemis from Apolla's home at once."

Karsh's protest about how difficult that would be right now fell on deaf ears. Ileana's second order — arbitration. A calling together of the Coventry Island Unity Council, the forum designed to settle community disputes and reduce endless rounds of magical showdowns.

Tonight's counsel, which had begun at the stroke of midnight, just might, the wizened trickster knew, seal Artemis's and Apolla's fate. It was at such a tribunal fourteen years ago that a decision about their birth mother had been made. It had been, Karsh reminded himself, the right decision, the only decision. He could only hope the Council would make as wise a choice today.

He was apprehensive but grateful for the chance to put his and Ileana's conflict before an impartial, wise, and learned group. It was his best shot. For, as much as it pleased him that the vain young witch was growing more powerful, she was still unpredictable. And could stoop to gravely misusing her magick. Had she not already nearly turned him into a frog?

Karsh wanted to believe that Ileana's heart was in the right place, that she truly felt separating Artemis and Apolla meant keeping them safe. Still, he was just as sure, had actually always known, there was no way to keep them apart. It was their birthright to be together, their destiny. And their best chance of survival. He only hoped he could make his argument strong enough so that the Council would agree with him.

Rhianna was speaking to the assembly. "You will now turn off all cellular phones, laptops, pagers, anything that beeps, burps, bounces, or vibrates." She stopped to take a breath.

"What's next, put your tray tables and seat-backs in their upright position?" Ileana snorted under her breath. "I hate this 'hocus-pocus-can-we-all-just-focus' stuff."

Ignoring the remark, though she had certainly heard it, Rhianna continued, "All herbs will now be tucked away, all candles snuffed, stones and crystals stuffed, all extrasensory powers suspended —" She stopped, and looked around the auditorium. "In other words, people, cease and desist the practice of all magick. Now."

With that, Rhianna settled herself on the plush, high-backed armchair in the center of the room, and motioned for Karsh and Ileana to take their seats.

As was customary in settling disputes, opposing parties sat facing each other on either side of the Exalted Elder. Council members took up the first several rows of the stadium. Interested onlookers filled the remaining seats. And today, the house was packed.

In front of each council member, a computer on which to cast their votes had been installed. Karsh had his doubts about decision-making by mouse, but the computers were gifts from a billionaire software warlock who lived in Silicon Valley. They were supposed to ensure quick and accurate balloting.

Though conflicts were settled by a majority vote of the council, an Exalted Elder always presided. The position rotated among the community's most esteemed and practiced members. It was the leader's responsibility to interpret the vote of the Council, and, if necessary, impose a course of action. At this phase of the moon, the Exalted Elder could have been one of two, Lord Grivveniss or Lady Rhianna.

Ileana, Karsh knew, had been banking on Grivveniss. And not just because of some unpleasant history between herself and the plump and dumpy Rhianna.

Karsh chuckled, remembering how the toddler Ileana had once described Rhianna as "the potato lady." He'd tried to shush her, but the willful child would not be quieted. "She's brown and round and has dimples just like a spud," Ileana had proclaimed, insisting Karsh agree with her.

Unfortunately, little Ileana had blurted that aloud in front of Rhianna, who'd never forgotten. Or quite forgiven her.

"For the Council's consideration," Rhianna now announced, "I give you the topic at hand. Our esteemed tracker, Karsh" — a smile escaped her lips as she nodded in his direction — "and the guardian, Ileana" — now the smile was gone — "wish to bring a conflict of grave and immediate importance before the council. It is regarding the twins. Apolla and Artemis — or Camryn and Alex, as they are now known."

From the back of the theater, an angry voice bellowed, "They should never have left the island! Where are they, Karsh?"

Instantly, Lady Rhianna rose from her seat and glared at the heckler. He was young, for all his bluster. He was, Karsh realized, the boy who'd pursued him in the woods. His name was Sinon.

"I warn you," Rhianna was saying, "I am the only one in this room allowed to use her powers. I can mute you if I have to, or turn you into anything." She threw a sidelong glance at Ileana. "Even a potato," she noted sourly, then continued. "There will be no outbursts or interruptions. These proceedings will continue in an orderly and fair fashion."

As she spoke, Karsh looked around the auditorium. He wasn't surprised to see that every seat was filled.

Word of this emergency session had spread quickly and, through his spies, Thantos kept in close touch with what was happening on Coventry Island. He still had family and sympathizers here. In truth, no one really knew who sided with the powerful warlock. Although most witches, and particularly the ones living on the island, were exceedingly trustworthy, there were always some whose allegiances could be bought and sold.

Sinon, the boy who'd shouted, was apparently one of them.

Pity. Karsh rubbed his forehead. Surely he knew by now that Artemis had left Montana.

But did he really believe that Karsh would reveal her new location, that a mere boy could track or trick him into revealing the whereabouts of Aron's daughters?

It was bad enough that Thantos had found them at the theme park — and it was all Karsh could do to get rid of him there. He'd heard the dark warlock had made an appearance at Artemis's trailer, too. Imagine if he'd found the grieving child!

Luckily, Karsh had acted quickly and she was long gone by then.

Rhianna had finished reminding the Council of its responsibility. To Karsh and Ileana, she said, "I will now give each of you time to state your position and make your arguments. What is the root of the dispute?"

Karsh winced at the creaking noise his knee made as he slowly stood. "Exalted Elder, wise members of the Council, fellow witches and warlocks, let me assure you that both I and Lady Ileana have the best of intentions regarding Artemis and Apolla. We always have. We only differ now in how to best protect them." He cleared his throat. "In light of certain new circumstances, that is."

As Karsh spoke, Ileana sat like a sulking child, arms folded, bee-stung lips firmly pressed together. Which didn't stop her from interrupting Karsh.

"He went behind my back," she accused. "He acted without regard for my wishes."

Karsh sighed loudly. "As I have explained, the situation was dire, and you, my dear, were not around."

"Then you should have waited until I was. I am their guardian."

"As I am yours," Karsh reminded her gently.

"Apolla and Artemis were separated as infants for their own well-being, for their protection," Ileana loudly announced. "They were dispatched to safe homes, homes with protectors —"

"Which I found for them," Karsh reminded the Council.

"So you did. And now it's you who have engineered their being together." Ileana stood, and faced the crowd. "They are not safe. Evil forces are afoot, forces wishing to bring harm to them. They must be separated. That is my contention, and it must be yours," Ileana finished with a dismissive wave.

Now Lady Rhianna clapped her hands, and took command of the amphitheater. "Let us recap, shall we? Artemis and Apolla were born to two of our most beloved and powerful practitioners of witchcraft. No one really knows what they can do together, only that their potential is infinite."

"I've seen them. They are quite amazing," Karsh confirmed.

"Tell us more, good Karsh," Rhianna commanded, intrigued.

"Oh, right. Tell us more, good Karsh," Ileana echoed irritably.

"Well, I am their tracker, of course," Karsh explained. "I've have been watching them all their lives —"

"At my request," Ileana noted.

"Recently, they met. No one is quite sure how. It could have been a random occurrence or Thantos may have lured them —"

The protests Karsh had expected broke out. "Leave Thantos out of this," one of the powerful warlock's followers demanded. "Lord Thantos would not harm them," another vowed. "He doesn't even know where they are!" This last, sullenly, from Sinon.

"Even so." Ileana's shrill shout silenced Thantos's followers. "They didn't have to be brought together. Karsh did that."

"How could I not?" he objected. "One had lost her protector. The other suspected she'd been adopted. Besides, they'd already . . . well, let's just say they'd tested their joined powers — and neither was likely to forget that."

"What exactly did they do?" Lady Rhianna asked, curious.

Karsh's pale eyes filled with pride. "You should have seen them. They were quite wonderful. Actually boss. The total bomb."

"Boss, bomb?" Ileana sneered. "Those expressions are older than you are, Karsh — as if that were possible."

The aged trickster ignored the insult. "They kept a family from falling to certain deaths," he continued, ardently. "Comforted a distraught child using an incantation —" He stopped himself lest he let too much slip. "But here is what's important. Everything they did was rooted in a heartfelt desire to help people."

Now Ileana exploded, "And in doing that, they put themselves in harm's way. He will find them!"

Being defensive would do nothing for his case, Karsh knew. Quietly, he asserted, "I gave Artemis tools with which to protect herself."

Ileana rolled her glorious gray eyes. "You gave her a few incantations. As if that will be enough."

Now Karsh couldn't contain himself. "Which she taught her sister immediately. Which — have you not been listening? — they've already used to good purpose."

Lady Rhianna now rose from her chair, levitating and rising above Karsh and Ileana. "Listen to me, both of you. Karsh . . . being the elder here, you should know this. When twin infants are separated, they lose much of their inborn ability. When they meet for the first time, there is an initial jolt of electricity — a bursting firecracker of energy — which creates the illusion they are fully powered-up, that their gifts are at full capacity. But without training, without guidance, that first burst will fade. Do you understand me?"

"Fade how? What do you mean?" Ileana asked.

"Until the twins are initiated, properly guided, what

they can do will be only the most elementary magick. For all you know, Karsh, their abilities may already be ebbing."

Ileana tried to contain the fear in her voice, but Karsh recognized it. "What powers will they be left with?" she asked.

"Oh, they will have some abilities they were born with, but they will not be as sharply attuned. They will not be able to control them. Their efforts at practicing the craft, dabbling in magick, may go wildly awry. Without protection, they'll —"

"But they have protection," Karsh interrupted. "I gave Artemis her necklace, the gold moon charm her parents blessed before —"

"Before," Rhianna broke in, "the unfortunate occurrence —"

"Before Thantos murdered their father!" Ileana shouted, setting off a wave of troubled grumbling in the great hall.

"I gave her the necklace," Karsh called above the uproar. "And I . . ." He looked down, away. He couldn't face Ileana now. "And I never took Apolla's away. She's had it since she was an infant. Wearing them will offer some protection —"

Ileana was livid. "Are you mad? Old trickster, don't you see? By their necklaces, Thantos will know them.

Every time they use their powers, it will bring him closer to them."

"He's already seen them together," Karsh was forced to confess.

"You don't know him," the boy Sinon called out. "He means no harm —"

"*You* don't know him," Ileana snapped.

Now Lady Rhianna lifted herself higher above the amphitheater floor. She shook her outstretched arms, unfurling a magnificent set of amber wings. The crowd grew still, then burst into applause at the impressive sight. "Enough," she quieted them. "We've heard enough. Until Lord Thantos himself appears before this Council —"

"Which he will never do," Ileana insisted.

"Then find him, bring him to us," Rhianna silenced her impatiently. "The Council will now vote. Should the twins, Artemis and Apolla, be separated, as is the demand of Ileana, or allowed to remain together, as Karsh contends?"

Karsh nervously scanned the theater. How many here were his friends, how many his foes? He watched as the Council members pressed the keys on their computers. This was how Apolla and Artemis's fate would be determined? Through these gadgets, devices, contraptions, these bizarre boxes. A slip of the mouse, a finger pressed on delete — or worse — and he'd have to abide by the Council's decision.

They were bent over their screens, their monitors; fingers clicking feverishly on their keyboards, mouses — or was it mice — gliding on foam pads. He couldn't tell if a quick decision was good or bad.

But swift it was. It came to Lady Rhianna telepathically. Her smile tipped Karsh off, allowing him not triumph but only a moment's relief.

"The Council has voted. I'm pleased to say I agree with the consensus." Rhianna peered down her stubby nose at Ileana. "The twins are to remain together."

Ileana's hands balled into fists at her side — which was quite a lot better than her waving them in an attempt to turn Rhianna into the potato she now only resembled. But, barred from using her powers, all she could do was fume. Which she did bountifully.

"It seems, Ileana, that you will have to finally do the job for which you were chosen," Rhianna said.

Instantly, Karsh came to Ileana's defense. "May I remind the Council that Ileana was but a child herself, barely seventeen years old, when she was given the responsibility for the infants."

The Exalted Elder grinned broadly. "Well, she ain't seventeen no more."

That did it. Ileana flew off the handle. "I don't have

the time or the clothes! What are they wearing in Marble Bay, anyway?"

The minute it came out of her mouth, she realized her slip. So did Karsh. If any of Thantos's friends were present — and at least one, the boy, was — they now knew where the twins could be found. Ileana lowered her head, ashen and ashamed.

"My dear, you should be delighted." Rhianna had floated down to ground level and was standing, with folded wings, directly in front of Ileana. "For, in fact, you were right. You came to this Council asserting your position as Artemis and Apolla's guardian. And so you are. Their guardian, teacher, protector, and mentor. When they come of age, it is you who will preside over their initiation. For fourteen years you've had little to do. Which, as far as I can tell, has suited you fine. Clearly, the situation has changed." She looked from Ileana to Karsh and back again. "I suggest" — she grinned — "you both get going."

CHAPTER THIRTY
BEYOND THE GATES

"I know what you're thinking," Cam said as they retrieved their bikes from the rack outside Music & More.

"Give me news, not history," Alex murmured. Even though she was doing it, too, it was still weird knowing someone could hack into her brain as handily as the FBI had tracked down the M & M computer. "And?" she challenged.

"And I disagree. I don't think she did it."

"I assume we're talking about Tonya?" Alex asked, mounting Dylan's bike.

"I keep telling you, she's got issues. But that doesn't make her a kidnapper."

"Okay, let's review," Alex suggested as Cam hopped

on her own wheels, and they hit the bike lane, side by side. "The police know that 'Devoted's' deranged letters were e-mailed from Music & More's back-room computer."

"And they think," Cam reminded her, "it was Kevin who sent them — since he works there, and is now MIA. Besides, he's a skeeve."

"Didn't you hear what the clerk had to say? Skull-boy could barely turn on the PC, let alone compose fan mail."

"Says your love puppy," Cam grumbled.

"And," Alex ignored the remark, "we know there's a Kevin–Marleigh connection because Jenny saw him with the diva."

They stopped at the four-way traffic light, but kept up the convo. "Okay, so Jenny saw a skull-earring-wearing creep hangin' with Marleigh —"

"And didn't tell anyone because she disobeyed her mom, and she got Marleigh's disappearance all mixed up with her little act of defiance," Alex continued. "Jenny thought she caused it. Her mom warned her that bad things could happen if she left her seat. And she left her seat and, boom, a bad thing happened."

"Marleigh got kidnapped," Cam completed the thought.

The light changed. "Which way to Tonya's?" Alex

asked, pulling away the minute Cam said, "Straight ahead."

"Okay." Cam caught up with her. "How about this? How come, if skanky Kev was in the middle of kidnapping Marleigh, she had time to scribble an upbeat autograph for Jenny? How come she didn't just scrawl 'Help!'?" Cam shook her head. "I don't know. It doesn't sound like Marleigh was being forced into anything."

"Yo, Nancy Drew, if Kevin's not 'Devoted,' then who is?"

"Okay, Harriet the Spy, make a left up the hill," Cam instructed. In her head, she knew Alex was right. Tonya had to be involved. She was the only person with a clear connection to both Kevin and Marleigh. But in her heart, Cam couldn't believe the forlorn girl could be so cruel. "Tonya's pathetic, not psychotic."

"Well, riddle me this, Batgirl," Alex huffed, pedaling up the steep incline that led to The Heights, Marble Bay's most exclusive area overlooking the water. "As we mentioned before, why was Tonya able to get cell phone reception up in the stands when, supposedly, Marleigh couldn't? And who was she talking to?"

Cam's eyes began to sting as the question echoed distantly in her head. Who *was* she talking to? All at once, her sight went blurry. The street became a kaleidoscope of signs, cars, houses. Her eyes began to water. And a hazy image came at her. She saw a craggy-faced boy with slicked-back hair, a skull earring dangling from one ear.

Shuddering, Cam shook her head, trying to clear her sight, rid herself of the leering image. Her bike veered crazily to the left, into the traffic lane. "Kevin," she said aloud.

"Excuse me?" Alex asked.

"You're right." Cam gripped the handlebars, adjusting her direction. "She was talking to Kevin."

"And you know that because?" Alex sounded amused.

"I saw it," Cam stammered faintly. "I mean, I just . . ." She cleared her throat. "I just know, that's all."

Up ahead a crowd milled in front of the Gladstone mansion. TV trucks were parked outside the tall iron gates surrounding the property, and the sidewalk was crisscrossed with cables. A police cruiser was rerouting traffic around the area.

Cam and Alex biked up to the officer in charge, a friendly-looking older sergeant with wisps of white hair showing under his police cap. Something about him seemed odd, yet strangely familiar. But neither Cam nor Alex had time for reflection right now. Marleigh Cooper's life was at stake, and they believed Tonya Gladstone could unlock the mystery. "We're friends of Tonya's," Cam told him. "Is there any way we can get to see her?"

On the hood of his car lay a clipboard, Cam noticed, holding a list of names. "'Fraid not," the policeman said with a genial smile. "No through traffic here. You gotta go down around Bailey Road."

"But Officer," Alex whined in a brokenhearted voice Cam had never heard her use before. "She's, like, so expecting us. Tonya's our best, our bud, our true-blue soul mate, and she urgently needs our support." What's she doing, Cam wondered — giving a lame imitation of how she thinks we sound here in Marble Bay?

Cam zoned in on the paper attached to the clipboard. There were eight names listed. Four of them with check marks behind them, four without. Her head hurt as she squinted harder at the list. Effie Trimble, Tonya's housekeeper, was one of the unchecked names. E.C. Rawlings was another.

"I mean, if she were your daughter," Alex pushed on, ignoring the feeling that both she and Cam *knew* this cop, "wouldn't you want her just surrounded by the people she loved?"

The policeman took up his clipboard, leaving Cam with a blurry smear of print and a throbbing headache. "Names?" he asked.

"I'm Effie and she's E.C.," Cam cut in quickly. She heard Alex's startled intake of breath, and then heard her saying, "That's E.C. for Elaine Charlotte. That's me. Elaine Charlotte Rawlings."

The officer seemed amused, then glanced at them warily. "Oh, yeah? How come you got different last names?" he asked.

"It's a long story," Alex answered.

"We were separated at birth," Cam volunteered. "Adopted by different families."

Looking suddenly sheepish, the officer cleared his throat. "Okay." He checked off the names and signaled to a raven-haired young woman cop at the gate. "They're okay. Let 'em in."

"That was too easy," Alex said suspiciously. "That cop . . ."

"No, I'm just brilliant," Cam assured her.

As they made their way through the crush of reporters and photographers, a grumbling rippled through the crowd. "Hey, that's not fair. We've been waiting here all night. Who are they? Why are they going in?"

A guy in Levi's shoved a mike in Cam's face, hollering, "You a friend of Tonya's or what?" A flashbulb went off, startling Alex.

"Move back, let them in, give them air," the captivating, dark-haired policewoman urged, wading through the reporters toward the girls. "Back off," she warned the frenzied journalists.

Alex blinked up at her, seeing her own face reflected in the officer's big, dark glasses. "Leave the bikes here. And you be careful," the cop commanded, "if you know what's good for you."

Shooing away the clamoring crowd, the stern policewoman brushed against Cam. Instantly, Cam felt a tingling current streak through her, a bolt that raised goose bumps on her arm.

The gate behind the officer was ajar. Out of the corner of her eye, Alex noticed a reporter slip through it and race behind a clump of hydrangea bushes. "Come on." She signaled Cam, who had stopped suddenly and stood rubbing her arms as though she were chilled.

The sound of Alex's voice got Cam going again. She hurried after her look-alike, running across the well-tended lawn of the Gladstone estate.

As they passed the stand of hydrangeas, the reporter Alex had glimpsed ambushed them, shouting out questions.

"Hey," Cam cried. "You're not supposed to be here."

Alex looked back, and he snapped her picture. She saw starbursts of color, the effect of the blinding flash. And then she saw Camryn, hands on hips, glaring at the pricey lens of his gazillion-dollar camera.

Still, when the explosion came, Alex was shocked.

The lens shattered, spewing glass, and the camera blew up in the sneaky guy's hands. And Cam could not conceal her glee.

Alex could. She quickly rang the bell. At once, the front door opened. A tanned, slim woman, her hair perfectly poufed, her nails bloodred, peered down her narrow nose at them. "Do I know you?" she asked, her manicured hand clutching the collar of her silk shirt.

Immediately, from the street, a blaze of flashbulbs and camera lights went on and questions were desperately shouted from the sidewalk.

"I know them, Mom," they heard Tonya say. "It's okay. Can they come in?"

Cam and Alex had only caught the briefest glimpse of Tonya's mother, but it was enough. The wealthy woman was ballistic, furious at the inconvenience her daughter had caused. She clearly cared little about Tonya herself.

"I'm sorry, Mother," Tonya wailed after her mother had stalked away. "How would I know she'd be kidnapped? I didn't know it would turn out like this," she snuffled.

"Really?" Alex asked casually. "How'd you think it would turn out?"

Tonya teared up, but didn't speak. Alex read her thoughts; they were loud and clear.

Well, for sure, I didn't expect that moronic slacker, Kevin Bullock, to take it out this far.

"Kevin? What about him?" Alex said, adding, "You know more than you told the police, don't you?"

Tonya was bright crimson, flushed from crying. Smears of eye makeup washed across her round, red cheeks. "What if I do? It doesn't matter now," she whined. "I can't believe what's happening to me. This is a total nightmare! And I just want it to end!"

"Happening to you?" Alex asked. "Interesting spin. Most people have this, I don't know, *weird idea* that it's happening to Marleigh."

Alex's sarcasm flew right over Tonya's head. "That's the worst part," she cried. "I just love her so much. I'd never have done anything this terrible, this, you know, like, real."

"So you might just pretend you were kidnapping her?" Alex asked.

Tonya's mouth fell open; her eyes widened with terror. *You know?* she asked.

Alex nodded.

"We do now," Cam said.

CHAPTER THIRTY-ONE
TONYA'S TALE

Alarmed, Tonya screamed, "But I didn't say that aloud, did I? I'm losing my mind!"

"How could you have heard me?" Tonya was trembling in Cam's grasp.

"Why don't we get out of the hall," Alex suggested. "Where's your room?"

"My rooms," Tonya emphasized the plural, "are upstairs." She led them along a sweeping staircase and down a corridor the width of Alex's trailer.

Then opening a paneled door, she showed them into her quarters, three rooms in all, a sitting room, bedroom, and a bright, lavishly sky-lit bathroom so filled with plants that it looked more like a tiled greenhouse.

Tonya flung herself onto a chintz-covered divan in the sitting room and laid back dramatically, like an exhausted empress. "Help me, please. Oh, please. I never meant for this to happen," she bawled. "It was just this stupid idea I had. I wanted to spring this ultimate surprise on you guys — well, not you," she said to Alex. "I mean, I didn't even know you, right?"

"Right, sure," Alex replied. "And the surprise was?" she prompted.

"Marleigh, of course. Marleigh Cooper. I knew if I got her to show up for the game, everyone would be so pumped. So I called —"

"And invited her," Cam prodded.

"Sort of. I mean, she's the Youth Spokesperson of this foundation. You know, One Last Wish —"

"That's for seriously ill kids, isn't it?" Alex asked.

"I suppose," Tonya said.

"You told her you were sick," Cam guessed. "That's what Marleigh meant when she said it was so tragic, wasn't it? You told her you were dying."

"Bone cancer," Tonya confessed, tears welling up again from her red-rimmed eyes. "And . . . sort of, like, uh, my leg was about to be amputated."

Alex shuddered at the word *cancer,* thinking with a rush of fear that her mother might die. Then she remembered that Sara *had* died. For a moment, grief took her breath away.

"That's why you were limping around on crutches," Cam was saying.

"Well, I did sprain my ankle a little during practice, remember?" Tonya got defensive.

"Oh, yeah," Alex growled at her. "Sprained ankle, cancer, I can see the similarities."

"You lied to Marleigh," Cam said. "You told her you were dying, didn't you?"

"Just to get her to come to Marble Bay," Alex added, not bothering to hide her disgust. "Just to show off for a bunch of spoiled —"

"Your teammates," Cam interrupted sharply. "I can understand that. You were trying to impress us, so you —"

Tonya caved. It was like, Alex thought, watching an iceberg melt all at once or a sand castle implode. "I wanted everyone at school to see that I can be cool. But I also did it for me. Marleigh and me."

Through a torrent of tears, Tonya poured out her whole story.

She honestly believed that if Marleigh got to know her, they could be total buds. So she'd concocted this "innocent" plan, to have Marleigh "pretend" kidnapped. "Just for a day or so," she'd put it, as if that made it okay!

Then, Tonya would rescue the singer, and Marleigh would be so grateful, they'd be bff's.

Of course, Tonya had needed help. It came in the shady form of Kevin Bullock, the Music & More slacker. He'd been the one allowing Tonya use of the back-room computer. For a fee, that is. And for an even bigger fee, he'd agreed to help Tonya carry out her whack kidnapping caper.

Cam suddenly had a chilling thought. She glanced quickly at Alex, wondering if the same thing had occurred to her. Or whether, annoying as it might be, Alex had figured it out first and "sent" the idea Cam's way.

"The demented fan," she mouthed silently to Alex.

"'Devoted,'" Alex's lips moved at the same time.

"It was you," they both said aloud, staring hard at Tonya.

"So what? There's no law against fan mail, is there?" Tonya insisted.

"No, of course not," Cam assured her.

"But there is against kidnapping," Alex warned.

"Okay, okay. I sent the letters," Tonya said. "And, for your information, they were not crazy or demented like people are saying, just emotional, like me. I'm a very emotional person. I e-mailed them from Music & More because I didn't want to send them from home, because my parents might find them."

Tonya barked a bitter laugh. "Like they'd be interested in anything I do. But they check their e-mail while they're traveling, and they know my password."

"Forget that," Alex demanded, impatient now. "So you're saying Kevin did exactly what you paid him to do — except he forgot the 'pretend' part and kidnapped her for real. How'd he do it? And more important, where is she?"

Tonya's tale continued. Cam thought it was sad; Alex thought it was pathetic.

Just as they'd planned it, Kevin had called Tonya on her cell phone at the soccer game. Tonya had then told Marleigh that a car was waiting to take her to the airport — that the singer had been a great sport to come to the game, but it was okay if she left now. Marleigh had been relieved to do just that.

So she'd left the stands not to take a phone call, but to go to her car. It was there, all right. Kevin was the driver. The singer had only paused long enough to give little Jenny her autograph. Then, she'd walked right into the trap Kevin had set for her.

"Where is she?" Alex continued. "Where'd he take her?"

"Is she . . . do you know if she's okay?" Cam was almost afraid to ask the question.

Tonya exploded, "I don't know! I don't know anything. All I know is what was supposed to happen. There's this old gardener's cottage way out back. It's got no phone and the electricity's turned off. I was going to, like, hide Marleigh there, and then I'd find her, you know? I'd rescue her, save her life. And she'd never forget me. She'd be my friend forever."

"But Kevin didn't go along with the game plan?" Cam pressed.

"He got all greedy," Tonya sniveled. "He took her someplace else. I don't know where and he won't tell me. He just keeps asking for more money. But I don't have any left and I can't ask my parents for more —"

Tonya was tearing up again. "Easy does it," Alex offered, awkwardly patting her shoulder. "We'll find her, right, Cam?"

Cam looked spacey. She was squinting at something behind them, something that was obviously giving her a headache. "Ow," she murmured, clutching her brow.

"I wanted to go to the police right away," Marleigh's would-be rescuer babbled on. "But I couldn't. And when they came after me, I wanted to tell them what happened. Except Kevin said not to or he'd spill his guts, tell how the whole thing was my idea. And everyone would know. My parents, the kids at school, all the reporters who interviewed me. Worst of all, Marleigh would know. That's something I could never face."

"You okay?" Alex asked Cam, who was still gazing into the distance, her unfocused eyes beginning to water.

"Camryn?" Tonya had noticed Cam's odd silence.

"Yes. What? I'm okay." Finally, Cam shook her head, which was still aching. "I know where he's hiding her," she said, blinking hard at Alex. "An old gas station with rusted pumps in front of it and wooden boards over the windows. It's, like, all overgrown with vines, lots of trees, and prickly bushes —"

"You rock," Alex cried out, punching the air with her fist. "Where is it?"

"That's the glitch," Cam said. "I don't know."

CHAPTER THIRTY-TWO
A LITTLE HELP FROM A FRIEND

"Great. Now what do we do?" Alex threw up her arms and flopped onto the divan.

Tonya stared at Cam with a look of horror. "Um, uh, what just happened?" she asked, slurping back her tears.

"She had a vision," Alex answered, too deep in thought to come up with a more creative reply.

"Excuse me?" Tonya's cow-brown eyes were as wide as they could get, given the pillows of puffy flesh surrounding them.

"She's kidding," Cam said quickly. She was still feeling a little woozy.

"Just kidding," Alex agreed. "But, hey, I've got the kick idea. Tonya, it's time to give a little shout-out to your partner-in-crime and make him an offer. You do have his phone number?"

"Beeper," Tonya said. "And I resent —"

"Excellent," Alex cut her off. "How 'bout you tell skull-boy you've got his money, but you'll only give it to him —"

"If he lets you see Marleigh," Cam finished the thought. "Because you're worried about her and want to make sure she's safe, right, Als?"

"No Marleigh, no money. That's the deal, Camille," Alex confirmed with a grin.

Buried in her tote bag, Cam's cell phone rang.

Alex heard it first. Still impressed with her new and improved hearing, she put her hand to her brow as though she were concentrating deeply, and said, "It's Kevin."

"Really?" Cam heard the ring, and fell for it. With shaking hands, she fished out her Nokia and checked the callback number. "Not," she announced, her eyes blazing at Alex. "It's Beth. Like that creep would even have my number." Cam hit the TALK button.

"Hey, hi. Where are you?" her best bud wanted to know.

She was primed to tell her when Alex shook her head no. "What's up?" Cam responded instead.

"Is this Camryn?" Beth asked grumpily.

"Beth, it's me. The real me. And I can't talk right now. We're, like, in the middle of something huge."

"We?" Beth repeated coldly. "Oh, you mean you and the girl you thought, a week ago, looked nothing like you? Sorry. My bad for crashing your private party."

It was the wrong time and place to mend fences, Cam realized, but the hurt in her best friend's voice was too painful to ignore.

"Beth," she said gently, walking away from Alex and Tonya into the mammoth bedroom. "I'm at Tonya Gladstone's house. She messed up big-time. She's in terrible shape." Cam considered issuing a warning, begging her best bud not to repeat what she was about to hear, but she stopped herself.

She didn't need a spell to seal Beth's lips or an incantation to assure her loyalty. From the get-go, Beth had seen herself as the wind beneath Cam's wings, the true-blue bud she could totally count on.

Elisabeth Fish was the one person in the world who'd come close to filling the empty feeling that had haunted Cam all her life, she realized now; the feeling that she was incomplete; that despite all the love, attention, and material goodies her parents had given her, something was missing.

That the missing something might turn out to be Alex Fielding didn't change the fact of her friendship with Beth.

Speaking of loyalty, Cam thought, where was her own? "Bethie," she whispered into her cellular. "She just, like, 'fessed up. Tonya. She's involved in Marleigh's kidnapping. She and Kevin Bullock — from the music store."

"O.M.G.!" Beth blurted. "How do you know? I mean, did you call the police? Should I?"

"Not yet. I'm afraid if we do that, something bad might happen to Marleigh. I mean, if it hasn't already . . ." Cam trailed off.

"So, what are you going to do?" Beth asked.

"I'm not sure," Cam admitted. "I have an idea of where Marleigh might be. Sort of. Some old, abandoned gas station out in, like, the middle of the woods, I think. It's all overgrown with vines and these sharp, shiny-leafed bushes —"

"Holly," Beth said. "There's loads of it growing wild out on Endicott."

"Endicott Drive?" Cam repeated. The vision she'd gotten in the CD store, of the word END, flashed in front of her. It had been only half the street sign, she realized now.

"Endicott near Webster Road," Beth was saying. "I think I know the place you're talking about, too, from when Sukari and I did that science project on indigenous plants. You know, like, what grows locally."

Instantly, Alex was at Cam's side.

"We went out on Endicott to collect holly. I remember that filling station. It's about thirty miles out and it was ultimate cruddy."

"Thirty miles from here to Endicott Drive?" Alex said.

"Endicott?" So much for privacy. Tonya, depressed and disheveled, was standing in the doorway now. "That's out near where Kevin lives," she said.

Cam hurried over to Tonya's phone and held the receiver out to her. "Go on, beep him," she said for the third time.

"I can't," Tonya wailed again.

"Oh, man. Not more tears," Alex grumbled. "I'm going to need hip boots if she doesn't stop soon."

Cam handed the phone to Tonya. "Please. We're only trying to help."

"I'm going to go to jail!" Tonya howled.

"No way," Alex promised her. "Cam's dad's a lawyer. He'll get you off. Right, Cam?"

"Dial!" Cam said, not knowing who she was more peeved at now, Tonya or Alex.

In the fifteen minutes it took for Kevin to return the page, Cam called her parents. It was only a little white lie, she rationalized, to tell them she and Alex were at Tonya's — and get their permission to stay the night.

Call-waiting clicked in just as Cam was saying good-bye. She nearly forgot she was using Tonya's phone and answered it. But magic or mojo, she remembered in time to hand the phone to the strange girl.

"Um, hey, hi, Kev," Tonya said. "Okay, okay. I beeped you 'cause now that my folks are home, I can definitely get the money you wanted."

"Only," Alex prompted her.

"Only, I'd like, you know —"

Impatiently, Alex scrawled TO SEE MARLEIGH!!! on the pad next to Tonya's phone and held it two inches from the girl's face.

"Um, to see Marleigh, you know? I mean, to see if she's okay and all." Tonya waited for Kevin's answer, then went, "No dice? Oh, uh, okay then."

Alex grabbed the phone, held her nose to imitate Tonya's weepy, congested voice, and said, "Then no Benjies, babe, no money. Unless I can check Marleigh out, it's over, Kevvy!"

Then she slammed down the phone.

"Oh, no," Cam groaned.

"Why'd you do that? Now he's gonna tell on me!" Tonya cried, heading straight for hysterical again.

Alex waved her off, predicting, "He's going to call back in a . . ." The phone rang again. "Half second."

She held her nose again and picked up the receiver. "Kevin? How did I know it was you? ESP," she said, rolling her eyes. "I can talk to her on the phone? Are you with her right now? No? You're not? Well, that's not good enough," she insisted. "I want to see her —"

Suddenly, Cam grabbed the phone from Alex. Speaking in a nasal whine remarkably like Tonya's, she said, "Okay, I'll settle for talking to her. When and where?"

Alex heard the treacherous boy's response. It had a tinny sound to it, like pebbles twanging on cheap metal. It would take him a while to get hold of a mobile phone, he complained. Sure, he'd ditched Marleigh's. Did she think he was dumb or something?

"If he were any dumber, he'd have to be watered twice a week," Alex whispered.

And then he'd have to go down to where "the package," as he called it, was stashed. So, it'd be an hour, maybe two, Kevin estimated, till he could tell Tonya where to meet him with the money.

Before Alex could seize back the phone, Cam said, "Okay, then. I'll be waiting," and hung up.

"Is it time to up your dosage?" Alex was furious. "You just lost it for us."

"No, I'm a genius," Cam answered, grinning broadly. "I just bought us an hour's worth of snoop-around time out on Endicott Drive."

CHAPTER THIRTY-THREE
BREAKING OUT

"Hello, Houston, we have a problem," Alex said as Cam did a little victory dance around Tonya's sitting room. "How are we going to get there?"

"Bikes, of course," Cam answered too quickly. Then she stopped abruptly. "Ooops. I see your point. Thirty miles by bicycle —"

"How fast brilliance fades," Alex noted.

Peeking out the window at the press corps kenneled behind the Gladstones' gates, Tonya added her two cents. "And how are we going to get out of here without being hassled by a million people? And that's not even counting my parents."

Cam's cellular jingled again. Deflated, she checked

caller ID, recognized Beth's number, and hit TALK. The first thing out of her best friend's mouth was, "Hey, how are you guys going to get out to Endicott? I mean, it's too far to bike."

Cam groaned. Alex laughed. Tonya, who hadn't overheard Beth's end of the convo, was ringing her hands, and droning, "We've got to find Marleigh. And I have to be the one to save her. It's the only way I can prove how concerned I am about her safety and happiness. Kevin's gonna tell everyone I planned the whole thing. He'll totally trash me. I'll be sent away — if not to prison, then to that dumb prep school that might as well have barbed wire and bars —"

"Put a sock in it, Tonya," Alex commanded. The desperate girl's soliloquy was making it hard for her to pick up Beth's voice. She guessed Cam had just asked her bud if she had any transportation ideas, because, tuning back in again, Alex heard Beth say, "Sure. Got brooms?"

"Yeah — and black capes and pointed hats," Cam replied dryly. "Come on, Beth. We've got about an hour to do this thing."

"Have you eaten yet?" her best bud asked.

"No," Alex shouted. "Tell her to send over a pizza."

Beth heard her. "Talk about mojo! That's just what I was thinking," she responded gleefully. "Just make sure it's from Pie in the Sky, and my friend—Jason — delivers it. Just try and remember his name —"

"El-is-abeth!" Cam broke her name into three distinct syllables. "We've got to get to that garage fast. This is not the time for a hookup."

"Hello! C'mon, Cam, give me some credit, huh? I was just thinking, Jason could drive into Tonya's with a pie and — ta-da! — drive *out* with you guys. I'm pretty sure he's working tonight. And don't jump down my throat, but I know he'd do anything you asked."

Alex grabbed the phone again. "Brainstorm!" she shouted to Beth. "We owe you, big-time."

"Yeah?" Beth laughed. "Think you can get Marleigh's autograph for me? I mean, if she's not too busy escaping. And," she added somberly, "if she's still . . . alive."

"Maybe we should have notified the police," Cam whispered to Alex as they and Tonya hunkered down between racks of warm pizza in the back of Jason Weissman's delivery van.

"Too late now," Alex reminded her.

Peering out the back window, Cam caught a glimpse of the old sergeant and the young policewoman. They were both watching the van pull away. Cam ducked down again. When she next looked out, a minute later it seemed, the pair and their black-and-white police car were gone.

Beth's estimate was on the money. They were trolling down Endicott, a seedy no-lane dirt road, twenty minutes later, and, shortly after that, stopping at the corner of Webster.

"I wish I could wait for you guys," Jason apologized as they piled out of the van. "How are you going to get home?" he asked.

Cam patted her tote bag. "Got my trusty cellular —"

"And her trusty daddy," Alex added.

Jason still hadn't gotten over the shock of seeing double. "Well, good luck," he said, not sure which Cam he was talking to.

The deserted filling station was a few yards away. All crumbling cement, boarded-up windows, and rusted pumps, it was nearly hidden behind a web of thorny vines and bushes. In short, to Cam's delight and amazement, it looked just like she had pictured it.

"I can see why the place is deserted," Alex commented as they picked their way through the tangled underbrush. "There're no houses, no people, no cars around. The only thing new here," she noted, reaching the shabby building, "is this."

A gleaming lock bolted the front door.

Cam tugged at it, to no avail.

"We don't even know if she's really in there," Tonya whined, anxiously looking over her shoulder.

"No, I guess the shiny, new combination lock is to keep out squirrels and raccoons," Alex murmured.

"Oh, it's a combination lock," Tonya cried, eyeing it now. "I'm pretty good at opening those."

While Tonya twirled the lock, listening intently for the right combo, Cam and Alex crept around to the side of the building and tried to pry a board off one of the windows.

The wood, old and rotten as it was, wouldn't budge — except to inflict splinters and cuts, of which neither girl wanted to be the first to complain.

"Is she even in there?" Cam asked, frustrated.

Alex rapped on the boards, calling Marleigh's name.

Cam stared at the unyielding plywood. "She's there!" she whispered, tugging at Alex's arm. "I can see her, through that little space in the boards."

"The only thing spacey around here is you, dude. The window's got no spaces or knotholes. It's your mojo to the rescue again. What do you see?"

"Marleigh," Cam answered, "but she's not moving. She's gagged and blindfolded and tied to a chair."

"Gagged? I knew it," Alex exclaimed. "That's why I couldn't make out the words."

"You heard her?" Cam demanded. "That means she's alive!"

"I heard something, but it was all muffled." She put her face close to the decaying wood. "Hey, hi," she called awkwardly.

"Marleigh!" Cam pushed Alex out of the way. "We're here to rescue you. Hang on. We've just got to break through this window."

"You shoved me," Alex complained.

"I'm sorry, but you were all, 'Hey, hi,' like we have time to chat."

Alex sneered. "Scorch it. The board. Scorch it, Cam. Use that flamethrower power of yours to get us in."

"I'm not sure I can," Cam whispered.

"It worked with that picture on your wall," Alex reminded her."

"Yeah, but I was really, really angry at you then. I mean, red-hot raging, burning mad."

"Well then, you spoiled rotten brat, you pathetically clueless boneheaded geek, loser —"

"Shut up!" Cam ordered, steaming.

"Don't waste your batteries on me. The window. Do the window," Alex ordered.

"But what if the whole place catches on fire before we get her out?"

"Melt the nails, demento dude! Do *something*, stooge!"

Unexpectedly, Cam grabbed Alex's hand. "You, too," she said. "Stare at them, you rancid, lame . . . I don't know!"

"Speaking of lame," Alex cracked, "you don't even have a decent supply of insults. Remind me to share —"

"Shut up and stare," Cam ordered.

Two nails had begun to heat up. A third, the one Alex finally focused on, was wiggling violently.

Then, *ping*!

"Duck!" Alex hollered as the bottom nail flew off.

"Get back!" Cam commanded as the top two nails melted, dripping molten metal down the front of the boarded-up window.

They tugged off the plywood. "Should we call Tonya?" Cam asked.

"No time," Alex insisted, scrambling to climb through the broken window.

Marleigh Cooper was a mess. When Cam finally made it inside, with Alex's grudging help, she had to stop herself from gasping.

The beautiful young singer's face was gaunt, streaked with tears, and mottled pink and white as though she'd had an outbreak of hives. Her once-flawless blond mane hung matted and greasy. Despite the tumble of fast-food cartons on the floor around her feet, Marleigh looked painfully thin and weak.

One of the ropes that held her to the chair was tied around her neck. Marleigh's pale skin was black and blue under the grimy cord.

If she had struggled any harder, Alex thought, *she might have injured her windpipe, and never been able to sing again.*

Or, Cam returned the thought, *she might have strangled herself.*

An orange glare poured through the busted window, a final blaze of dying sunlight. "Leave her blindfold alone," Cam told Alex. "Just until it gets a little darker out. She's probably been blindfolded for days. The light might hurt her eyes."

"Yes," Marleigh agreed in a pitiful whisper after Cam took the gag off. "Please, just untie me. Please."

Alex worked at the ropes as Cam whipped out her cell phone. The only thing that stopped her from calling the police was Tonya. If the cops came now, Cam and Alex would have to spill everything they knew: Ratting out Tonya in front of Marleigh was something neither of them could do. So Cam speed-dialed her home. "Oh, no. I can't believe it. No one's there," she said as the voice mail picked up. "Okay, I can deal. I'll call a cab."

She was dialing information, Alex was kneeling before Marleigh, freeing the grateful girl's ankles, when Tonya gave a bloodcurdling scream and rushed through the front door.

She was about to say something — when she spotted Marleigh. Tonya gasped, and fell to her knees. "It's me, Marleigh. Tonya Gladstone. Oh, please forgive me. I'm so sorry. I only wanted you to like me —"

The still-blindfolded singer reached out her newly freed hands. Her wrists were painfully discolored from the pinch of the ropes. "Tonya? Oh, I'm so glad you're here —"

As the bedraggled victim tried to comfort the girl who'd planned her kidnapping, Alex heard an unsettling noise. So did Tonya, who suddenly remembered why she'd come flying in.

"It's him!" she said, belatedly remembering to whisper. "Kevin!" He just pulled up on his motorcycle. He's gonna tell. Then everyone will know . . ."

Alex didn't need to hear the rest. She ran outside.

CHAPTER THIRTY-FOUR
FACE-OFF

A craggy-faced boy wearing a dangling skull earring was a few yards away from the building. "Who are you?" he called, shutting his noisy motorcycle and climbing off. "What are you doing here?"

He came toward her, swaggering, sneering. Alex saw a shadow fall across him. She looked up. In the fading twilight, she found the tree branch that shaded his angry face. It was big and high, and would certainly do serious damage if it crashed down. But it wasn't directly above him anymore. He'd walked past it.

Kevin stopped suddenly, still out of range. "What's going on?" he shouted, looking pathetically confused. "Hey, how many of you are there?"

Alex figured, rightly, that Cam had bolted out of the filling station after her. But would she see the problem?

She didn't want to take a chance and just communicate telepathically with Cam. The sitch was way beyond dangerous. "That humongous branch," she hissed, not taking her eyes off Kevin, hoping Cam heard her. "I think I can get it to break and fall, but it might miss him. He's got to move back about a foot."

"Can you really do that?" Cam whispered behind her.

Alex wasn't sure. Would she have to hold Cam's hand to borrow some mojo? She didn't have an incantation for this one — should she try to make up some weird rhyme? She hated how unpredictable her newfound gifts were. Could she pull this off just by wanting it to happen, concentrating hard enough?

Totally, she decided. Where had Camryn been when she'd sent that basketball hurtling into Ina's mouth or the peanut-butter sticky spoon flying at Beeson's thick skull? She hadn't known Cam existed back then. She hadn't even met Doc yet.

"If he'd just back up about a foot," she murmured.

"Speaking of foot," Cam said, with sudden, undisguised delight.

What seemed like a second later, the toe of Kevin's

sneaker sent up a suspicious smoke signal. Then it exploded in flame. The boy yelped and grabbed his ankle, hopping around, frantically trying to blow out the hotfoot Cam had obviously sent his way.

He hopped backward, Alex saw with glee.

She focused on the branch with all her might. She squinted and chanted silently, *Fall, fall, fall, please don't stall.*

Then suddenly, Cam's hand was on her back, sending an awesome chill down her spine. There was a creaking noise as the branch swayed, and then an earsplitting crack a moment before it plummeted.

"Bull's-eye!" Cam hollered as Kevin went down. "I did it."

"You did what?" Alex demanded.

"I stared at him, I locked eyes with him, that's what."

"And gave him a hotfoot. Big whoop. I made the branch fall."

"You guys got him!" Tonya had raced out of the service station after them.

"Love to debate who put the skankster out," Cam told Alex, "but there just isn't time. Tonya, stay here and holler if he moves, okay?"

"But I'm the one who's supposed to save Marleigh!" Tonya bawled.

"Yeah, but you're the best screamer we've got, so

you've got to guard Kevin for a minute, just until we finish untying her."

Cam was multitasking like mad, already dialing the taxi company, when Alex followed her back into the garage.

They stopped dead in their tracks.

Marleigh was right where she'd been before — only not just blindfolded. The gag was back in her mouth and her hands and feet were bound again. Her head had fallen back, as though she were unconscious.

"I felt the neck cords were a bit brutal," a man's deep voice said. "So I didn't replace those."

Alex and Cam spun around. Sitting on a rusty stool, in front of what was left of the station's counter, was a hulking, bearded man in a turtleneck sweater. His pant legs, Alex noticed, were tucked into a pair of thick boots far too heavy for summer.

Cam's eyes began to sting as she stared at the intruder. Alex's ears felt blocked, as if she were wearing earmuffs. "Who are you?" she asked, her own voice echoing in her head. "How'd you get in here?"

"You were at Big Sky, near the Ferris wheel, right?" Cam asked, squinting at him. "You're Mr. Sot Naht, aren't you?"

"How perceptive you are." The big man chuckled. "But you've got it backward, I'm afraid."

The boots, Alex thought, a vague recollection nagging at her suddenly tired brain. "Where did you come from?" she asked, her voice breaking embarrassingly.

"The question I should think," the man said slowly, smiling a smart-alecky smile, "is where did you come from?"

His glittering black eyes pinned Cam. Instinctively, she covered her own eyes. "Good reflexes," the stranger noted.

Cam felt the blood drain from her head. Woozy, she almost collapsed. Her cell phone went clattering to the floor as she grabbed the back of Marleigh's chair for balance.

Alex, too, felt lightheaded. With great effort, she tried to remember what it was about the man's boots that gnawed at her weary mind. Then, all at once, it came to her.

Though he looked nothing like Beeson, she knew: "You're the one Lucinda and Evan were talking about, aren't you?" she asked, stunned. "You're the one who was looking for me at the trailer. You stomped right through the floor."

"What are you doing here? What do you want?" Cam asked.

But the man was staring at Alex now. "What is that abomination you're wearing?" he bellowed, pointing at

Evan's gift. "That tawdry trinket." Then he turned back to Cam. "Where are your necklaces?" he roared.

"The chain's busted," Cam stammered. "I broke it accidentally."

"What necklace?" Alex asked.

The man shook his head disapprovingly. "She would be heartbroken if she knew."

"Who?" Alex asked, her mouth dry as dust.

"Your mother!" the man replied, angrily gnashing his teeth. "I have a message from her."

"My mother is dead," Alex told him defiantly.

"Who is she? Where is she?" Cam asked.

"She lives. And needs you. And only I can take you to her —"

"In a pig's eye, buster!" The beautiful young officer, who'd stood guard at Tonya's gates, crashed through the door, her gun in two hands, pointing at the invader. "Hold it right there!"

"Ileana, my dear. How well you look." The huge man stood and bowed gallantly.

"The Council has decreed that you must appear in person," the policewoman barked at him. "Let's get going."

"But you've done a marvelous job," he crooned lazily. "These children are exceptional. My compliments."

"Let's go, move it!" the officer insisted. "My partner and I are empowered to take you into custody —"

"Karsh?" he thundered. "My *old* friend?" He emphasized the word *old,* then laughed meanly. "Your partner, is he?"

"Yes," the officer called Ileana said. "He's waiting for you outside. I'll join you in a moment. I need a word with these reckless children."

"Very well," the big man said cordially, but his dark eyes glittered with danger.

Alex and Cam could hear him calling to the older man as he stepped outside. "Ah, Karsh, we meet again, you decrepit old warlock. I see your eyebrows have mended. I'd gladly set fire to your feet this time, if we were not in the presence of the fledglings."

They heard the old policeman chuckle. "Do not fear. You'll soon be out of their company. Forever," he promised in an oddly grating voice.

"Really, they make me weak . . . weak with yearning," the other man boomed. "Miranda would be so proud. Their gifts are quite extraordinary —"

"Gifts you'll never corrupt!"

He sounded different now, like someone from another time, Alex thought. Totally different than he'd sounded in front of Tonya's house.

Cam recognized the voice. It belonged to . . . was it possible? The strange man from her dreams?

"Hello. Excuse me. May I have your attention?" the

policewoman demanded. She whipped off her dark glasses and glared at them. "You think you're pretty clever, don't you? Clever and oh-so-special. Well, let me tell you something —"

Whatever it was she wanted to tell them was lost to the shock of seeing her eyes. Gray, they were, as distinctively sharp and silver-gray as their own eyes.

"Am I getting through to you?" Ileana demanded, kneeling now to undo Marleigh's ropes. The singer was moving, but not yet fully conscious. "You put yourselves in grave peril. That man who was in here a minute ago, he's dangerous. Seriously dangerous."

"And crazy, too," Alex added. "He said he could take us to our —"

"Maybe he's not crazy," Cam broke in heatedly. "Maybe he really does know where she is —"

"Yours, maybe. Not mine," Alex argued. "I only had one mom, and I know exactly where she is."

"Enough!" the policewoman boomed. "Artemis is right. The man is mad. A dangerous maniac."

Alex and Cam looked at each other. "Artemis?" Cam said.

"I meant Alex. Of course," the officer quickly amended. "Stay away from him. Both of you," she admonished them. "If you ever see him again — run. Just run, fast and far. And don't think those paltry powers of yours are going to constantly get you out of scraps. You're young. You're vulnerable —"

A loud noise, a sonic boom, ripped the air, stopping her midsentence. She ran outside and left them staring after her.

Marleigh was coming to. In addition to removing the ropes, the policewoman had taken off her gag and blindfold.

"Are you okay?" Cam asked her.

The singer nodded and tried to stand up. She swayed and Alex caught her. "You're the girl from the soccer game, aren't you?"

"It's a long story," Cam interrupted as Alex lowered Marleigh gently back into the chair.

"Karsh?" they heard the policewoman call. "Where are you? This is no time for your tricks. Materialize!"

Suddenly, they heard a distant peal of delighted laughter from beyond the door.

"Just rest. You're safe. The police are here," Cam assured Marleigh.

"Yeah, we'll be right back," Alex called over her shoulder as they raced outside.

Night had fallen. There was a full moon overhead. It lit an odd scene.

Kevin still lay where he had fallen, but he'd been

tied up, trussed like a turkey, his skinny body wrapped around in vines.

More vines bound Tonya to the trunk of a tree, which was swaying wildly, though there was hardly a breeze to stir it.

Alone in the moonlight, Ileana stood before the tree laughing her silvered laugh.

"Old sorcerer," she seemed to be talking to Tonya, tied there. "How could you let him do this to you? I've half a mind to let you stay as you are. Where is he? What have you done with him?"

From the ground near Ileana's feet, there came a *hiss* and *whish* and a rustle of plants, sounds of a feral creature slipping through the underbrush.

Ileana leaped back. "A snake?" she scolded. "You turned him into a snake?! Why not a bird or a jet plane or a comet or something equally difficult to catch?"

"I think she's losing it," Alex muttered to Cam.

But Cam was staring transfixed at the swaying tree. "Alex," she said in a squeaky whisper, "there's a man in the tree."

"No way," Alex said, squinting hard through the moonlit gloom.

"No, not up there, not on a branch. He's actually in the tree. He's . . . uh-oh . . . pasty-white and bony and . . ."

"Doc?" Alex thought she recognized a face.

"The bleacher-creature," Camryn breathed.

The man in the tree winked at them. Then Ileana whirled around. "Oh, for pity's sake," she said, staring at them reproachfully. In a flash, she whipped out a pouch from her pocket.

The last thing Cam remembered was something that looked like green flakes being tossed in her eyes.

The last thing Alex remembered was a familiar, fragrant smell. And the word *skullcap*.

Distant sirens woke them some time later.

CHAPTER THIRTY-FIVE
WHAT ARE WE?

Camryn Barnes used to think her life was an open book, a story full of certainties and absolutes. With sentences that ended in periods.

So past tense.

In the space of a few short summer weeks, her autobiography had flown open to a whole new chapter. One that was full of uncertainties, mysteries. With sentences that ended in question marks.

Before Alex — the source of all those questions — had come into her life, Cam hadn't spent a whole lot of time by herself. There were always friends around or on the phone, family, activities, school — just stuff.

On those super-rare occasions when she really did

need to be alone, to think, scribble in her journal, listen to music on her Discman, she would bike into the center of town, and then hike up a hill in Mariner's Park. She took the same trail every time to the same secluded spot.

It was no big deal, really. Just a patch of grass under an ancient elm tree that offered an amazing view of the harbor below. It was usually really quiet, and there was little chance of running into anyone she knew.

Cam didn't think of it as her sanctuary exactly, just as a place that felt familiar and comforting.

No one in her family, none of her friends — not even Beth — knew about the site.

At twilight on the day after they'd rescued Marleigh Cooper, she took Alex there.

Under the sheltering branches of that elm, the two girls sat, so strangely alike yet very different, hugging their knees, staring off with their amazing black-rimmed gray eyes toward the harbor below. For the longest time neither spoke.

"It's pretty cool that your dad's going to take Tonya's case," Alex finally offered.

When Cam didn't respond, Alex continued, "Probably her parents could've speed-dialed some high-powered superlawyer to represent her and make the whole mess go away. At least Dave will make sure Tonya gets the help she needs. He's a really nice guy."

"A nice guy," Cam repeated, lost in thought. "If only he'd been nice enough to tell me the truth, before I accidentally bumped into it myself."

"The stealth-adoption thing rears its ugly head," Alex commented.

"I know you went through a lot," Cam said, her voice breaking, trying to get past the lump in her throat. "And my own stuff can't really compare to it. I just never believed they'd lie to me like that. Especially not him."

Alex shrugged, and plucked a blade of grass. "You, of course, have never lied to them."

"No," Cam said defensively.

"Oh, then I guess you've told them about knowing things before they happen, and having visions, and, um, melting bolts —"

"Point taken," Cam interrupted. "And don't bother reading my mind. I'm not going to tell them. Ever fill your mom in on how you can hear thoughts, and make things move just by thinking about them?"

At the mention of Sara, Alex mellowed abruptly. "No," she whispered. "But in a strange way, I always had this feeling that my mom knew. Look," she added, "probably neither of us should say anything yet. To anyone. I don't know."

"I don't know," Cam repeated the words slowly. "That defines my whole life right now."

"And mine," Alex reminded her.

"Als? What do you think that guy meant when he said —"

". . . She lives? And only I can take you to her?" Alex finished the sentence, then unclasped her arms and stretched out on her back. The bristly grass, still warm from the day's heat, prickled against her spine as she thought about the creep with the thick-soled boots. He'd said a lot of things — told them to wear necklaces, which was too strange, as though the dude was into accessories. Plus he knew the blond officer by name. But it was his fiery rant about a woman he insisted was their mother that haunted both of them. Something Alex adamantly refused to consider.

"I have no clue," she answered Cam, "about him or about that policewoman. What's her deal? She had . . ."

"Our eyes," Cam finished. "I know."

"And how'd she know my name?"

"She called you Artemis. That's not your name," Cam reminded her.

"Actually, she corrected herself. She called me Alex. Which neither of us told her."

"No. In fact, we gave the old cop phony names, remember? E.C. and Effie, to get through Tonya's gates."

"The white-haired cop," Alex mused, "who transformed black-beard —"

". . . who looked a lot like that guy whose place we stayed at in Montana, into a snake."

"Before turning himself into a tree." Alex stopped herself. "Know what we sound like? Candidates for the insanity defense, right behind Tonya."

Cam leaned back next to her. "Okay, I plead mental and emotional overload. But eyes on the prize, I guess. Marleigh's safe, Tonya's going to get help —"

"And all's well in your world. And that, ladies and gentlemen, concludes our special episode for the night."

"My world," Cam responded, ignoring Alex's sarcasm. "It could be your world, too."

"No way," Alex said, thinking about the call she'd gotten earlier. The one she'd been hoping for.

Lucinda and Evan had heard her name on the news, they said. And so had Andy Yatz and Ina Barrow and everyone in Crow Creek. And they were all so proud of her. They were calling from the library where Mrs. Bass had let them use the phone.

Alex fought back tears talking to them, thinking of Mrs. Bass and the musty old library where Sara had taken her for story time when she was little. She promised to write home soon. Or e-mail them at the library, which Mrs. Bass had said would be okay with her.

She'd already said good-bye for the third time, when it hit her. "How'd you get this number?" she asked Lucinda.

"This big guy who owns a ranch about twenty miles from Big Sky — he came to the park. We were all talking about you, you know. And how wc wished we could reach you. He said, try information. Ask for the Dave Barnes residence over in Marble Bay, Massachusetts. So we did."

"What big guy?" Alex asked, but Evan had taken the phone from 'Cinda and hollered, "So long, Alex. We'll be e-ing ya!" and hung up.

"If you give them a chance?" Cam broke into Alex's reverie. "I'm not saying the people in my world, my friends, can replace your friends, but there's a lot to like about them," she was saying. "Beth already likes you."

"Right. Like Beth even knows me. I'm just the hick who invaded your clique."

"She doesn't think that, and neither will the others."

Alex sighed again. "Look, your friend is majorly weirded out by me, but what is she gonna say? Flip it over for a sec and think about if *Beth* suddenly came home from vacation with a look-alike sister. What would *you* do?"

Cam considered. "I'd be polite. And welcoming. But in my heart, of course I'd want her . . . twin person . . . to stay. I mean, now that they'd finally found each other. Not that they knew they were looking. Come on, you know what I mean. She should stay. *You* should stay."

There, she'd said it.

But Alex shook her head. "No. This isn't my park. This isn't my tree. Or my town. And the words 'Seven Pack' don't exactly roll off the tongue. This isn't my life. No matter what the dippy DNA thing says."

Cam sat up and hovered over Alex. "Even if it turns out, beyond a shadow of a doubt, that we *are* identical twins? Born of the same parents? Whoever they are — or were?"

Alex set her jaw and looked out over the harbor. "It doesn't matter."

"It's *all* that matters." Cam came right back at her. And then she added, because suddenly it was clear to her, as if by magic, she knew exactly what she wanted to say and what Alex wanted to hear, "Alexandra Nicole Fielding, please stay. I want you to live with us. I want you to be with me and my family and my friends. I want them to be your family and friends. I want that more than I've ever wanted anything in my entire life."

Alex shook her head, but when she looked at Cam, her eyes were sparkling mischievously. "So, Camryn Alicia Barnes. You want me to stay. More than anything in your entire life. More than a shopping spree? More than a convertible when you turn sixteen? More than a whip-fast laptop with DVD player? More than — oh, I don't know — an amazingly cool itty-bitty superpowered StarTac cell phone?"

Cam's eyes glittered right back. "Not more than the cell phone."

And then they burst out laughing. Peals of laughter echoed around the park, seemed to bounce off bushes and trees, rocks and hills. Their laughter tickled blades of grass and drifted over the harbor, all the way out to the bay where, like mist, it floated toward the sky.

That night, by the light of the moon, the face, the man, came to her again as he had when she was a child. It was the same face she'd seen at the soccer game, pale and wrinkled, but it no longer frightened her.

In her dream, Cam welcomed him. When he spoke to her, she answered.

"Free them from blame, Apolla. It's time to forgive. And to trust," he said.

"Trust?" she'd responded angrily, knowing that he'd meant Dave and Emily Barnes. "How can I? Why should I? They never told me the truth."

"Truth?" The face seemed to soften, and now looked almost kindly. "There are many kinds of truth. These good people have sheltered you, and cared for you, and loved you unconditionally. They have kept you safe and would do anything to make you happy. That also is the truth."

Cam had no response to that.

"These people, Apolla, have enough love in their

302

hearts for all of you. For their son, for you — and for Artemis."

Cam knew he meant Alex. Suddenly, in her dream, she asked, "Why are you calling us those names? Apolla — the name you called me when I was little. I don't know who I am."

"But you will, I promise you. Honor your parents. Put on your necklace. Do not forget."

Alex was visited, too. By the man who'd transported her two thousand miles in a single day. Doc. That he would come to her in her dreams didn't surprise her. He seemed to know exactly what was on her mind, and he spoke gently to her.

"I know you miss her. You will always miss her."
Sara.

"Remember that she loved you, she was your protector. And you gave her the greatest happiness of her life. But you couldn't have saved her. It was her time. Free yourself from blame. Take her love with you, and start a new life. Artemis, precious child, your real life has just begun."

Then he winked. "And, trust me," he said, laughing suddenly. "It's gonna be interesting. Catchya later, Als."

Artemis. He'd called her that before — it still puzzled her.

 303

But when he called her Als, it tickled her. She smiled in her sleep.

That morning, at exactly the same moment, Camryn and Alexandra awakened. If they'd stolen a glance at the night table between their beds, they would have seen things that had not been there when they'd gone to sleep.

On Cam's side, next to a tiny bouquet of sweet-smelling green leaves with gay purple heads, was her half-sun necklace. The chain she'd angrily torn had been replaced by a new one of shimmering gold.

On Alex's side, in the silk-covered box that Doc had given her, was the half-moon necklace.

Had the girls tried to put them together, they'd have seen how perfectly the two shapes fit, how they matched to form a complete circle.

There was a note, too, written in beautiful calligraphy, lying between the necklaces. It read, HE MADE THEM WITH HIS OWN HANDS. SHE BLESSED THEM WITH HER BLOOD. THEY WANTED YOU TO WEAR THEM ALWAYS.

They would find and wonder about these gifts later. But for the moment, as the first ray of sunlight streaked through the blinds, something else was on their minds.

Cam was first to speak. "What do you think we are?"

"What do you mean?" Alex replied.

"You know. We're identical. We can do all this stuff that no one else can. We can help people. We can make magical things happen — and see things and hear things and make things and people move. Als, do you think we might be witches?"

Alex turned to face Cam. Their extraordinary gray eyes locked. "You want to know what I think? Read my mind."

And so Cam did. "Wait," she said, "I'm getting mixed messages here. I'm not sure whether you're thinking, 'Twins.' Or 'Witches.' 'Cause it came out 'T'Witches.'"

"Exactly," Alex said.

CHAPTER THIRTY-SIX
SAFE AT HOME

It was midnight when Karsh and Ileana, exhausted and exhilarated, got back to Coventry Island and arrived at Ileana's cottage. The temperature had dipped well below freezing, and the old trickster could see his breath as he tried to speak. Correction, he could see what breath he still had. Rescuing the twins had taken its toll on him.

With a rush of pride, he regarded Ileana, at his side now, still in her police uniform. She'd been absolutely brilliant today. She'd proved the Council's decision of fourteen years ago a wise one. For she really was up to the task of guarding and guiding Artemis and Apolla.

"That was fine work you did today," he complimented her.

"Necessary — thanks to you," she grumbled, whipping off her policewoman's cap. "Do I have hat hair?"

Karsh beamed. "Your hair, my dear Ileana, is perfect. As were you. You rose to the occasion."

Ileana sighed deeply and collapsed on her front steps, displacing the sleeping Boris. "Look, Karsh, I never wanted them together. Now that they are, 'the occasion,' as you call it, will rise again and again. It will be harder and harder to protect them."

"Ah, my good-hearted but crabby crone, it really is too late to undo what's been done. As they grow, with our help, their powers will get stronger. More important, they'll learn how to use them."

"You wanted me to see them for myself. Well, I did. And here's what I saw. Two cocky kids who think — in the vernacular of the day, old man — that they are *all that.* They solved a mystery; they found Marleigh Cooper. And it was easy! So they think they're invincible. But in a face-off with Thantos, they'll be quickly rendered powerless."

"That's where we come in — just as we did today," Karsh reminded her.

"What part of this don't you get, Karsh? Thantos has seen everything we have. The nerve of him — to confront them! To tease them with talk of Miranda. He is shameless."

"The Council will have something to say about that," Karsh reminded her.

"If he acquiesces and stands before them. Is there any power on Earth that can get him to do what he doesn't want to?"

"I'm sure there is," Karsh said mysteriously.

"I don't know what you're referring to, and I'm really far too exhausted to debate this." She stood abruptly. "I'm going in. But let this be a parting thought. He knows where they are. He doesn't work alone. He's got allies, who will come to them in various shapes and forms. The twin daughters of Aron and Miranda will be tested every single day."

"Then we'll have to be more vigilant. But these girls — we're going to have to get used to calling them Camryn and Alex — deserve to have a life, a home, a family, friends. They deserve to have some sense of normalcy and happiness, as they grow toward fulfilling their destiny."

"Their destiny! You keep talking about that. You're still not seeing it. Now that they are together, in this normal life as you call it, it's not just they who are at risk. Thantos will stop at nothing. All those people around them, friends and protectors alike? From this moment on, no one is safe."

ABOUT THE AUTHORS

H.B. Gilmour is the author of numerous best-selling books for adults and young readers, including the *Clueless* movie novelization and series; *Pretty in Pink,* a University of Iowa Best Book for Young Readers; and *Godzilla,* a Nickelodeon Kids Choice nominee. She also co-wrote the award-winning screenplay *Tag.*

H.B. lives in upstate New York with her husband, John Johann, and their misunderstood dog, Fred, one of the family's five pit bulls, three cats, two snakes (a boa constrictor and a python), and five extremely bright, animal-loving children.

Randi Reisfeld has written many best-sellers, such as the *Clueless* series (which she wrote with H.B.); the *Moesha* series; and biographies of Prince William, New Kids on the Block, and Hanson. Her Scholastic paperback *Got Issues Much?* was named an ALA Best Book for Reluctant Readers in 1999.

Randi has always been fascinated with the randomness of life . . . About how any of our lives can simply "turn on a dime" and instantly (snap!) be forever changed. About the power each one of us has deep inside, if only we knew how to access it. About how any of us would react if, out of the blue, we came face-to-face with our exact double.

From those random fascinations, T*Witches was born.

Oh, and BTW: She has no twin (that she knows of) but an extremely cool family and cadre of bffs to whom she is totally devoted.

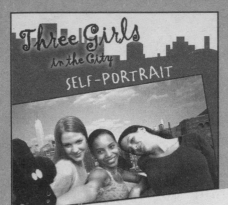